The Evolution

The Survive Saga, Book 2
Samuel Morris Jr.

Dedication

This book is dedicated to my wife Christina, my children Samiyah and Sammy, my parents Kimberly and Samuel, my siblings Daniel, Noelle, and Zuriel, my family, my friends, and my supporters.

Chapter One

Inside a log cabin in the woods at sunset on Christmas day 2049, thirteen-year-old Robert Williams sat on the living room floor, staring at the carving knife in his hand. He had caramel skin and light brown eyes. Robert was five feet three inches tall with a curly black afro.

He wore a black shirt, a charcoal jacket with scarlet mandarin letters on the rear, and black jeans. Since a little after midnight, he hadn't moved. All he'd done was cry.

The death of his mom was one of the main thoughts on his mind. Her boyfriend killed her after becoming a Reaper, a monstrosity with razor-sharp teeth and claws, an exposed jaw, and a muscular physique. Their skin glowed neon blue, and their entire eyeball was black. Reapers were one variety of Taken created by Mateo Hernandez, mutants who were human before getting bit on the neck. The moment his mother Candace Jenkins turned into one kept replaying in his memory. Her vacant, inky eyes stared right at him before General Johnson stabbed her in the head.

Robert's father, James Williams, opened his brown eyes and sat upright. He was a thirty-three-year-old African American with espresso brown skin. James stood around five feet eight inches tall with a low-cut fade and full facial hair. He wore a blue shirt, a black jacket with a thick cotton collar, and blue jeans. Robert scooted backwards away from him until he backed himself into the house's front corner and held the knife up.

James reached out a hand to him. "What's wrong?"

Sofia and Liam awoke. Sofia Hernandez was a twenty-nine-year-old Colombian with light tan skin and brown eyes. She was five feet one inch tall with black hair past her shoulders, plump lips, and a beauty mark below her left nostril. Sofia had on a sunset gold shirt, a pair of white jeans, and a brown hooded leather jacket.

Liam Smith was thirty-seven years old with beige skin and blue eyes. He stood five feet eight inches tall with brown hair, a full beard, and a mustache. Liam donned gray jeans, a red shirt, and a chocolate leather jacket with an upturned neckline. Robert looked from them to his dad. As James rose, Robert breathed hard. James took a step towards him, and Robert hyperventilated.

James halted. "What's the matter?"

He stared at his father with more tears streaming down his face. "You died."

Robert turned to Liam and Sofia. "All of you did."

James glanced at Sofia and Liam. She returned his gaze. He moved to his son, kneeled, and took the knife from him.

James grabbed his son's shoulder. "Are you sure we were dead? Maybe the Evolution formula incapacitated us."

Robert shook his head. "One hundred percent. I tried to wake you up, but you weren't responding. Then you stopped breathing, and I couldn't find a pulse. I did C.P.R., but it didn't work. You haven't moved since last night."

James headed for the window. The red glow of the setting sun painted the sky and the snow from the storm.

He leaned on the ledge. "So, you've been here by yourself for over twelve hours, thinking we were dead?"

James faced his son. Robert watched him. James' eyes watered. He held open his arms as he strode towards Robert. His child hugged him, and they cried.

James positioned his kid at arm's length. "I'm sorry you went through that. As your parent, I never should have endangered you by endangering myself. I was wrong, and I apologize. Do you think you can forgive me?"

Robert wiped his tears away. "Of course."

He paused. "You seemed dead. Thinking you would turn like mom scared me. I don't know if I could've stopped you."

James tried to respond but couldn't find the words. He pulled Robert in for another hug. After a moment, he released him and exited the cabin through the kitchen door.

Sofia strolled over to Robert and placed her palm on his shoulder. "I'm sorry too. What we did was reckless and unacceptable. We let the situation cloud our judgment. Wanting to stop my dad's monsters and my mother's powers made us desperate and stupid. We don't know how this ends, or how much time we have left. That's why we took a risk."

Sofia shook her head. "We intend to make certain you get to experience life for decades to come, and your father and I get extra years to live our lives together. I promise to do a better job of protecting him, even from himself."

She touched the side of Robert's face and smiled.

He returned a smile. "Thank you, Sofia."

She rubbed his cheek. "I'll check on him."

Robert nodded, and Sofia left through the rear door.

Liam approached Robert and patted his upper arm. "If the three of us die, there's one thousand dollars in my room. Change your name to Roberto and move to Mexico or anywhere in the southern United

Continents of America. The cost of living is superior there compared to the U.S.A."

Robert peered at him.

Liam smirked. "I'll leave the planning to your dad."

He watched the exit. "James will return any second."

Liam whistled and rocked back and forth. Robert walked away and relaxed on the couch.

Liam held his hand in the air. "Good talk."

He stopped whistling and rocking. Liam plopped down in his father's favorite chair.

***

Sofia moved onto the snow-covered deck. She shivered as her breath froze upon exhaling. Sofia rubbed her arms to fight the cold. James leaned against the railing.

He examined the night sky through the bare trees. '*What do I do now?*' he thought.

She went to his side and stroked his back. He turned and wrapped her in his embrace.

Sofia kissed his cheek and then his lips twice. "I almost lost you, just as things were getting interesting."

James chuckled. "Don't you mean beginning?"

She grinned. "Relationships are most exciting at the start. Unless you meet the one. Then they can be enjoyable later too."

He kissed her forehead.

James stared into her eyes. "If anything happens to me,"

She put her finger to his lips. "We won't speak that into existence. Let's just make sure we're all okay."

He sighed. "I can't believe we did that. We endangered ourselves and Robert. There is already enough trying to kill us. We shouldn't do the job for them."

Sofia nodded. He leaned backward against the railing.

She positioned herself in his arms and pulled them closer for warmth. "This feels nice. Way better than fighting monsters."

Sofia sighed. "We should disappear. Let Mr. White deal with this."

James smiled. "That sounds good."

She watched him. "You agree we should leave too?"

He gazed at her. "No. It seems great, but we must think long term. Although I would love to vanish and allow Mr. White to handle this, we need to do this. Which is why we drank the Evolution formula, and...I endangered my son. Do you want him to catch your parents after they've turned thousands of people into Taken?"

Sofia strode away from James to the top step on their right. "I'm unclear about who or what they are, given their actions. My dad is different. The man who raised me wouldn't have hurt anyone. He would never trade me for anything. What happened to my mother broke him. And my mama..."

He headed to Sofia and caressed her back.

She glanced at him. "I don't know what she is now. Is she part Taken, full Taken, or something else? I can't believe she's okay with what papa has done. When you offered to trade the formula for me, I saw she didn't agree. The mom I knew is still in there."

Sofia frowned. "Even after his experiments to keep her alive changed her, she is more human than him."

James took her hand. "Another reason we need to catch them. After what she did to General Johnson, Mr. White must be angry. We must locate them first so we can try to help your mother and stop them both."

She sighed. "My instincts scream we should drive off, but my gut tells me that won't end well. But if the real her remains inside, I must try to save my mom."

He lifted her chin. "There's so much at stake. I am doing this for you and Robert. He deserves a future, and I hope our relationship lasts longer than two nights. I don't plan to die filled with regrets because I waited too long to ask you. Old in my bed, happy, and content with a life lived to the fullest is the way I wanna go. The apocalypse shouldn't have made me recognize time is fleeting. It always was, is, and will be."

James caressed her fingers with his thumb. "If we run and Mr. White doesn't stop your father, no place will be safe. Our days with each other would be short as Taken spread through the continents."

Sofia looked over her shoulder as she went towards the rear entrance. "You're right. I wish we got together sooner, but I'm glad it happened at all. Let's plan our next move with Liam."

She opened the door, and he entered after her.

As they walked in, Liam sprang up and met them in the kitchen. He glanced at James. "Listen, I'm great with kids when I'm one of multiple adults. Those situations allow us to play zone defense. Robert's wonderful, but please don't put me in a one on one again. Man coverage isn't my strength. It's very much a weakness. I was so................... uncomfortable."

Sofia and James observed Robert sitting on the sofa and then looked at each other.

She stared across at Liam. "Something's wrong with you."

He raised his finger. "Agreed, but that's beside the point."

James and Sofia peered at him.

Liam rubbed his neck. "Haha, anyway... are you good?"

James grinned. "Yeah, I needed fresh air and Sofia's counsel."

Liam clapped. "Okay, great. While you were talking, I came up with an excellent strategy. First, we return to The Agency, knock out the agents with the automatic weapons and use their limp bodies to fool the security scanner in the main elevator. When we get to the main floor, James and I will throw them at the next two while you pound anybody else unconscious with a combo. Then I'll take point with both of you flanking me, and we'll defeat fifty to sixty people as we go to the armory. If Mr. White protests, he'll receive a pimp slap on our way out. After that, we track down your parents, shoot through a thousand Taken, kick in the door, then we bring them to justice. It's perfect, right?"

Sofia and James looked at him.

Liam studied them. "I see you're overwhelmed with my plan's..."

"Ridiculousness." She gave a disapproving look.

He chuckled. "What? You thought that was my actual idea? I was only..."

Liam glanced at the floor. "Masking my pain with humor. I'm angry about my dad. He threw himself into a crowd of Reapers to give us an opportunity to defeat Mateo, and we failed. We gotta complete the mission. For General Johnson, Colonel Brian and... my old man."

James grabbed Liam's shoulder. "We're going to finish this. When we capture them, where do we go?"

Liam scratched his head as he peeked at Sofia. "I haven't figured that part out yet. Anywhere else must be better than giving them to Mr. White and The Agency. I think the United Bureau of Investigation is more trustworthy."

He paused. "It didn't sound right in my mind, but I still said it. I thought it might seem decent out loud, but it didn't."

James faced Sofia. "So, I'm thinking we drive to the city. That's the direction their HoverCopter was going, along with most of the Taken."

Liam peered at her. "Are there any labs in town?"

She laughed. "Allegheny is one of the leading cities in the world for research. Downtown is the most popular location for the newer, well-funded laboratories. It's another way to have an 'ego' measuring contest."

James smirked. "Okay, we should get moving. After the physical and emotional exhaustion of yesterday, we recovered with a well needed rest. But after being out for almost eighteen hours, time isn't a luxury. We have the skeleton of a game plan. Let's put the meat on it as we go to town."

Robert got up when James, Liam, and Sofia walked toward the entrance. Liam poured water on the fire. The smoke replaced the flames' rhythm with its own. They departed the cabin and headed towards the white HoverVan. Liam hopped in the driver's seat. Robert entered the passenger side. Sofia and James sat behind them.

She leaned forward. "Should we be in here? Is it safe after we wore our suits in here yesterday?"

Liam eyed her. "Now you say something?"

He stared at James. "Between the Remnant shots, the bodysuits, and the sterilization fog at your dad's lab, we should be good. If not, I hope the formula gives us super immunity."

Robert peered at his father. "What about me? I didn't drink any of it."

Liam held up a hand to cut James off and looked at Robert. "If the worst should happen and you turn because of exposure, you'll be our Taken teenager. Or Tate for short."

Sofia pinched the bridge of her nose.

James eyed Liam. "You will be fine Robert."

Liam raised his hands. "I was trying to help."

She chuckled. "Try a little less."

He turned on the car. "I guess three is a crowd. Speeches are on you two going forward."

Robert watched all of them. "You were out for a long time. Do you feel any different?"

Sofia, Liam, and James all glanced at one another. One by one, they shook their heads.

Robert looked out the window. "It would've been cool if it worked."

James gazed at Sofia. "Yeah, it could've been."

Liam backed the van from its spot and shifted into drive.

He gripped Robert's shoulder. "Worry not, little Tate, everything's gonna be just fine from here on out."

Robert eyed him. "Please don't call me that."

Liam pulled his arm back. "Okay. Just trying it out. I see you didn't like it, and that's cool."

He continued to steer as he muttered to himself. "You'll always be little Tate to me."

Chapter Two

All was black. Fifty-seven-year-old General Oliver Johnson heard a faint sound. He turned his head, looking for its source. The General detected a clearer second beep. This time, louder and closer. He redirected his hearing again, but couldn't locate the noise's origin. The beeps intensified and increased in pace. His heart thumped faster. General Johnson gasped as he opened his dark brown eyes. Sweat poured down his clean-shaven face. He ran his right hand through his gray flattop. The General lay in a hospital bed. He looked to the right at the cardiac monitor as it beeped.

'*So that's what I was hearing.*' he thought.

The pace slowed as his pulse did. He glanced and saw cybernetics where his left arm and left leg used to be. The cybernetic arm met his alabaster skin at the shoulder while the leg joined at the hip. They constructed both appendages of carbon steel. A BrainLink implant controlled them while nano energy solar cells powered them. He tried to sit up, but his left side wouldn't move.

A physician entered the room and rushed towards him. "Please relax General. We can't have you falling to the floor."

General Johnson gripped the man's white coat with his normal muscular arm. "Get me Mr. White, now, or you will be the one having the accident."

He released the doctor, who darted away. The General grabbed his skull with his natural hand and squeezed his eyes.

Mr. White arrived. He was a forty-three-year-old with praline skin. Mr. White stood five feet eleven inches tall.

His hair was black and slicked back.

He had a five o'clock shadow and deep brown eyes.

Mr. White wore an all-black suit, dress shirt, and tie combo.

He shook his head. "Do not threaten my employees, Oliver. These scientists, doctors, and agents are the best chance we have to stop Mateo and Andrea Hernandez."

General Johnson swatted Mr. White's comment. "I'm the best chance you have. Please tell me why my cybernetics aren't functioning."

Mr. White snapped his fingers, and a technician ran to the computer. After a few moments at the HoloKeys, the blue lights started running down both cybernetic limbs. The tech exited at the second finger snap. The General pushed himself to a sitting position.

General Johnson was six feet tall. He rose and stretched his new appendages. "With these babies, I'll be quicker and stronger."

Mr. White took a cigar from his black metal case and lit it. "Without staff like the physician you threatened, you'd still be two-thirds of a man."

He puffed and exhaled. "So, don't threaten them again. It took too much work to acquire the personnel I have."

The General nodded. "The next time I see her, it'll be a fairer fight."

Mr. White chuckled. "Let's hope, for your right side's sake."

General Johnson walked to the window looking towards the researchers. "Where is she?"

Mr. White exhaled a puff of smoke. "Downtown Allegheny."

The General smashed his cybernetic fist through the glass, which sent shards flying everywhere. All the scientists' attention turned to the sound and the debris. The agents posted outside the room moved closer.

Mr. White put his cigar out. "Let's make something clear straight away. This is my house. Respect everything and everyone in it, or I will remove you. Don't get comfortable because of your position."

He paused for a moment. "I once had a best friend, knew him for twenty years since I was little. One day he crossed me because he'd fallen on challenging times. I gifted him everything I could to help him, and he still stole from me. If I dealt with him, I won't hesitate to deal with you."

He walked over to General Johnson and stood in his face. "Is that understood?"

The General gave an icy stare. "Yes sir."

Mr. White turned, and the hushed area filled with the sounds of work.

He looked back at General Johnson. "As I was saying, she's Downtown. The agents are stretched thin, searching the number of research facilities they might be in, dealing with thousands of Taken, and other issues. We're fighting on two fronts while overseeing special projects on top of our usual duties."

Mr. White placed his hand on the General's shoulder and scanned his eyes. "I can see you're ready to return to the field, but first I need to be sure you could handle the job. If I instruct you to bring them in alive, I must know that you'll comply. General Johnson stared at his technological fist.

Mr. White shook his head. "I understand what she did to you. What his monsters did to Brian. I must make sure that you focus your actions on saving the continents and not revenge.

The General sat on the bed. "My focus is the same."

General Johnson paused. "It's just hard when something so horrible happens to you, and the city you love, by a friend you were close to once. When we worked together, our bond was strong. Once Andrea was pregnant, things changed. I understood that. My priorities shifted when I met Shelley. She became the light of my life."

Mr. White nodded. "People and situations change. We must play the cards we have now and focus on winning the game."

He walked to the hole where the window used to be.

The General stood. "I take it you've enhanced Brian."

Mr. White smiled. "I have. If you are going to finish your mission, you'll need your second in command with you."

General Johnson looked at his enhancements. "This time, things are gonna be different."

Mr. White turned. "Yeah, they will."

He clapped his hands. "So, I have something to show you."

Mr. White snapped, and a couple of agents brought in a massive drone on a HoverCart. The General grinned.

Mr. White smirked back. "We finished producing these early enough for the next operation. I intended this as a surprise before all this happened. With the stakes this high, I'm happy we can test them."

General Johnson ran his right hand over the drone. "If Senator Pennell approved these two years ago, we wouldn't be here. We would've stopped the bombing on the North Side. They never would have hurt Andrea. Mateo would not have created those abominations, and I would not... have these."

Mr. White tossed the General a modified HoloWatch. "You were beholden to archaic procedures. I've studied the past and I embrace it, as I welcome the future. The Agency moves one thousand miles per hour towards it. To save this city and the continents, I'll do whatever it takes to achieve the goal. I know you shall as well. Just remember, we need them alive so they may reverse what they have done."

The General slipped on the watch. "Yes sir."

Mr. White nodded and exited the room. As he walked down the hallway from the science department through the agent section to his workspace, people moved from his path while avoiding eye contact. Mr. White entered his office and closed the door behind him. He removed his jacket and loosened his tie. Mr. White dropped three ice cubes into his cup and filled it with bourbon. He drank half the glass. Mr. White leaned against his desk and placed the drink beside him. He touched his HoloWatch, and a few seconds later, Madam President Mary Jacksonson's hologram appeared in front of him. She was an elegant African American woman in her early sixties. The President stood five feet two inches tall, with chestnut brown skin, shoulder length black hair, and brown eyes. She wore a red dress with a pearl necklace and matching earrings. President Jacksonson beamed at him.

He smiled back. "Mary, I've got an update for you."

Chapter Three

Colonel Brian settled on a plush black couch in The Agency's break room. The black-and-white floor was checker boarded with red walls, metal tables, and stools. He bit into a slice of meat lover's pizza. His body was muscular, his face was clean shaven, and his hair was short and jet-black. He wore his usual army outfit. Brian noticed Isaac staring at him seated at the table a few feet away. Isaac was heavier, shaved, with short gray hair. He wore a black Agency suit with a red shirt and black tie.

Brian finished his bite. "It's hard to eat when people are looking at me."

Isaac leaned forward. "How can you want food right now? Forget that. How are you alive? That Hunter killed you. Despite witnessing your death, here you are, devouring food in front of me. I know there have been exponential advances in MedTech, but nothing to this degree."

Brian dropped his piece of pizza onto the plate. "I was hungry, but now that you've brought it up, it's bothering me. Mr. White and the doctors told me I died. You confirmed it, and I remember dying. I recall being gutted by that yellow Taken. When I try to remember it, I see flashes of something else."

Isaac nodded. "Maybe your brain is blocking the memory out. Lord knows that's not an event I would want to recollect."

Brian shook his head. "Not my death. It's different."

Isaac checked for other agents. "What do you think you're seeing?"

Brian stared at him. "I have no idea."

He sighed. "I must speak to Mr. White about the side effects of whatever they did to me."

Isaac held up a hand. "Consult the physicians first. Even though I'm here, I'm skeptical of him."

Brian slapped the couch. "I already asked the medical team. They informed me that flashes are normal, and they should go away. What part of resurrecting someone is common? They say I shouldn't worry, but I don't believe them. The doctors know the issue."

Isaac frowned. "Give it a little time. Perhaps your mind needs to adjust."

Brian sat back in his chair. "You may be right. I mean, I was dead, and now I'm alive. I'll be thankful for that and make this second chance count."

Isaac leaned backward. "Let me ask you something. What's up with the digital psyches?"

Brian nodded. "At The Agency, we receive weekly assessments of our thought processes. That way, they can search for optimizations. Then we're trained to enhance those skills as agents."

Isaac scratched his head. "Is my brain supposed to itch?"

Brian pointed at him. "You'll get used to it."

He looked at Isaac and chuckled to himself.

Isaac mimicked him. "What's so funny?"

Brian smiled. "Seeing you in that suit is amusing. For over a year, I've attempted to convince you to join our organization. You've always denied me. The world goes to hell and poof, you're an agent. Why the sudden change of heart?"

Isaac reclined. "You know about the tradition in my family of Police Captains. Liam's a great kid, and I love him. I knew he had the ability, but I wasn't sure about his willingness."

He chuckled. "Almost everything is a joke to him. I hesitated to leave until he was ready to do the job. Perhaps I enjoyed being around him more than I realized and wasn't prepared to go."

Isaac stood. "Things happened that pushed me to get involved. We discussed him taking over for me again, and Liam accepted the offer."

His gaze met the ground. "After you died, the situation was dire. Mateo lifted the gates and Taken poured into the garage. We did our best to resist them, but they overwhelmed us. Closing the gate seemed like our only shot at completing the mission. Standing outside of the garage, I shot the controls."

Isaac looked at Brian. "I wanted to buy them ample time to try, even if I wasn't by their side. Reapers came from every direction. I took down several of them with headshots. One of my finest hours, until a Reaper pounced on me."

He shuddered. "It tackled me to the sidewalk, and I smacked the back of my helmet hard off the concrete. I'm certain I had a concussion. While I laid there in a daze, it positioned itself to bite my neck."

"So, how are you here now?" Brian interrupted.

Isaac continued. "At the last possible second, Mr. White's agents swooped in like a well-oiled machine and saved me. I've seen nothing like it. The precision, the decisiveness, and the grace. The medic in the squad examined me while others kept guard. A few entered the building. Minutes later, I saw General Johnson come out in terrible shape. Liam and the civilians weren't with him. A few more emerged with your body and put you into a Hover Transport Unit. Others carried tranquilized Reapers. I attempted to stand up to say something, but my head ached."

He closed his eyes. "I stayed there for a while with my eyelids shut. When I felt the explosion at ground level, I opened them and seen the General and a couple of people laid out. I forced myself to stand, and I went to check on him. Seeing him up close, I expected his imminent death."

Isaac paused. "His left arm and leg were gone, and his pulse was faint. The other two perished. I returned to the transport to get the paramedic who was checking on their four captured Taken. Behind me, I heard the van with Liam and the others speed away."

He shrugged his shoulders. "I guess they assumed I died. With the situation I charged into, who could fault them? I didn't know where they were going, and I couldn't follow them. The Reaper busted my communicator when it tackled me, so I couldn't call them. So, I returned with the agents."

Brian rubbed his chin. "Why did they capture four live monsters when we brought them seven corpses to study?"

Isaac shook his head. "That's a good question."

He leaned forward. "When we returned to The Agency, I was distraught. I tried to reach out to Liam using a new HoloWatch, but he didn't respond. My headache kept pounding, so I found an empty desk and rested. I woke to an agent standing in front of me. He informed me that Mr. White wanted to talk to me."

Isaac looked at him. "I had my reservations while we spoke. I'm still skeptical about trusting him. When he showed me you and General Johnson, it persuaded me to join."

He pointed toward the door. "He should be dead, and that Hunter killed you. Anyone who has the power to reverse death can stop Mateo and Andrea. Liam and the rest will be safe once we end this."

Brian placed his hand on Isaac's shoulder. "So, my best friend is in the field with me again. Just like old times."

Isaac chuckled. "Which old times? Being young troublemakers in the neighborhood? Our time together in active duty as soldiers traveling around the globe? Or when we were police officers before you returned to the army?"

Brian smirked. "All of them. When I re-enlisted in the military, I hoped you would re-enlist with me. Liam was still young, so I understood why you didn't. Then they charged your father with extortion."

Isaac rubbed his head. "Who could've imagined my dad was dirty?"

Brian looked at him. "Nobody would've thought it."

He smiled. "You fought through it though, and became an exceptional leader yourself. Now Liam will continue the tradition. I understand the importance it has for you, and I'm glad it's happening."

Isaac snickered. "In an alternate world, you could be the Captain. If Liam never accepted the job and you were still my partner on the force, I would've nominated you."

Brian disagreed. "To make sure the legacy continues, you would restrain Liam and make him comply."

They both laughed.

A thought occurred to Isaac. "Speaking of carrying on legacies, when was the last time you spoke with Emily?"

Brian stared at Isaac with his eyebrows furrowed.

Isaac held out his hand. "I understand you dislike when I mention her, but given the circumstances, I thought it was necessary to ask."

Brian sat back and averted his gaze.

Isaac let his palm fall to the table. "Liam's absence made me realize the importance of our kids in a crisis. I'm even missing his wisecracks. Emily is family to me..."

Brian started to speak but stopped himself.

He stood. "For now, let's focus on finding Mateo and Andrea. I should go check on Oliver and see if he's awake."

Isaac nodded.

Brian walked to the door and paused. "Can we ... talk about Emily later?"

Isaac gave a nod. "Of course."

Brian half smiled and left the lounge. Isaac sighed as he reclined in his chair. He checked his HoloWatch and called Liam. Once again, he got no response.

Chapter Four

At the edge of Downtown Allegheny, a white skyscraper loomed over the rest. During sunset, Andrea Hernandez stared into the distance from the window.

Andrea was a fifty-two-year-old Colombian with blue-green eyes, and light tan skin that had a dazzling white luminescence.

She stood five feet five inches tall, had a slim-thick physique with short curly black hair, and wore a white lab coat with an orange blouse and blue jeans.

Andrea blacked out the ShadeGlass windows to avoid revealing their position. She sighed and turned to her husband, Mateo, who was a forty-nine-year-old Colombian with tan skin.

He stood five feet eleven inches tall, had an average physique with black hair and brown eyes, and wore a black lab coat with rolled sleeves, a black polo shirt, and gray dress pants.

Mateo sat at one of the three giant square metal tables and worked in the dimmed light. In the room, several Evolved Thinkers, Hunters, and a dozen Reapers stood against the white walls.

She strolled across the white tile floor towards him. "How can I help?"

Mateo continued his work. "I don't need any help."

Andrea touched his back. "Are you sure?"

He glanced at her. "Positive."

She grabbed a HoloPad off the table and reviewed the notes.

Mateo placed down his holographic device. "What are you doing?"

Andrea stared at him. "Helping you."

He walked away. "You should've helped earlier and killed Oliver."

She shook her head. "I work as a Neural Engineer. Enhancing neural systems is my specialty. I devoted my life to aiding people, not harming them. Everything you are doing was supposed to be targeted. What you have done has not been. I did not agree to this. If you want his elimination, then do it yourself. I won't kill our friend. I'm not a murderer."

Mateo turned to face Andrea. "I'm a Genetic Engineer, and a killer."

He paused. "You know I took the lives of men as a teenager because they murdered my parents. After they were dead, I ran to your house to find you. We fled Colombia together and never looked back."

Mateo chuckled. "I was young and weak, unable to grasp the power of being the predator. I was afraid of it. All my life adults taught me that killing was evil. They never mentioned how powerful it felt. In hindsight, the learned shame motivated me to commit my entire existence to aiding the prey's survival."

Andrea shook her head. "Murdering is wicked. Not something to celebrate. It can change you if you let it."

He fixed his eyes on Andrea. "I am already transformed. The bombing last year reminded me I was still acting like prey."

Mateo paused. "I almost lost you. During that time, the United Terrorists Against America were the predators. I realized the power I had when we hunted the U.T.A.A."

He clenched his fist. "We reversed our roles. When the first terrorist agent became a Reaper, it made me recall who I was deep inside my soul. It evoked a sense of my true self. The one I tried to bury."

Her brow furrowed. "The real you is a great husband and father. Please stop this."

Mateo smirked. "You don't understand. The leader becoming the inaugural Hunter was ecstasy for me. I never wanted to lose that feeling. The only thing clinging me to normalcy was you and Sofia. Although I enjoyed being dominant, I wanted to relax and be happy with both of you. When Mr. White tried to murder us, it cemented in me that even if you're a hunter, you can be the apex predator's meal."

He slammed his fist into his palm. "I will be no one's prey again."

Andrea walked over to him and placed her hand on his cheek. "The man that I cherished and raised my child with is still in you. Do not let anger consume you. Avoid letting the actions of others dictate who you are my love. Fight to be who you are."

Mateo smiled as he touched her face with his hand. "You're not listening."

She pulled back from him.

He shook his head. "I have rediscovered who I should've been. For years, I've buried all anger and aggression dealing with this world. I always questioned my thoughts and feelings, but I knew who I was. My brain was trying to protect me from myself. Attempting to safeguard my family, I am fond of who I have become. What I was, hidden deep within since that day."

Andrea backed up towards the window.

Mateo smirked. "Most humans can take a life in specific situations. Many individuals wish to remove someone without consequences. The people who have murdered before drop anybody with less hesitation the next occasion it crosses their mind."

He shook his head. "The non-killers who ponder but don't act, they end up as the victims. My actions will help humanity. I shall exclude those not strong enough to survive the evolution."

She stared at him. "When were you going to tell me your plan changed? Did you expect me to follow your desires even if I disagreed with them?"

Mateo took a step toward her. "This was supposed to be targeted, but when you pull one weed, another replaces it. Removing evil individuals is necessary for a transformed world. I say we burn the whole damn forest down and see what rises from the ashes. In my estimation, it should be a more gracious and humbler species. A more grateful and transformed society, where survivors won't take their existence for granted again. A civilization composed of the smartest, the strongest, the fastest, and the most adaptive. Where we can be happy and thrive."

He advanced in her direction. "No, this wasn't in your plans. Ending Mr. White and those like him is the goal. I assured you I would handle anybody who played a role in the bombing last year. That's what I'm still doing. I thought you wanted that too."

Andrea held out her hand. "What I want is my daughter. I want my family back together."

She smacked the back of her right hand in her left palm. "We had a strategy. The U.T.A.A. members get mutated, and those accountable removed. How is turning innocent civilians into Taken justifiable?"

Mateo chuckled. "I revised the course of action to include saving the innocents from a fate worse than death."

Andrea shook her head. "What outcome is worse than death?"

He smiled. "Mediocrity. A mundane existence satisfies many. They think consuming whatever corporations pump to them through feeds and 'reality' entertainment is fulfillment."

Mateo sucked his teeth. "They are living a sham existence. Their lives were a waste of time. They were not living; just existing."

He analyzed the Taken in the room. "At least now they have a purpose. A meaning to why they occupy the space they do. They're contributing to society more than ever, bringing us closer as a species with each Taken. Some of them may have been racist and now stand next to those they discriminated."

She furrowed her brow. "This has gone too far."

Mateo shook his head. "This hasn't gone far enough... yet."

Andrea studied his eyes. "It was essential to punish the terrorists and those responsible for the bombings. This is different."

She pointed at him. "You lack the authority to decide someone's worth. Who are you to judge them?"

He stared at her. "Isn't it obvious?"

Mateo chuckled. "I'm the creator of life. The concluder of conflicts. This is the beginning of a new world and the ending of the old one."

He smiled at Andrea as she took another step back towards the window.

Mateo advanced in her direction. "You claim I am responsible, and when humanity benefits, the praise will be mine. I'll take the blame too, but don't give me that holier than thou crap. A certain someone was side by side with me, engineering the minds of Reapers, Thinkers, and Hunters. Keep in mind, it's your genetics that flows through all of them. They're your children too."

Andrea shook her head. "Not by choice."

He grinned. "There's always a choice."

She clinched her fist. "You didn't allow me to choose."

Mateo paused. "If you were so upset by what I did, why did you help me?"

Daggers flew from her eyes. "I did that because I love you. You are my husband, my everything. I'd do anything for you, then you turn around and throw it in my face."

Andrea studied him for a moment. "You'd just saved my life. I would've died had it not been for you. Anger consumed me too. The U.T.A.A. made me suffer, along with thousands of others."

She touched her chest. "Vengeance was on my mind, but the innocent did not choose to undergo change. I didn't ask you to change them, or to use my D.N.A. You were supposed to be running my labs to make sure I was okay, but you deceived me."

Andrea shook her head. "Your claim of altruism masks your self-interest. I helped you for the other victims and their families who couldn't fix an injustice. Being a victim of the bombing prompted me to think of our younger days in Colombia. I would not stand by while the terrorists took lives near me, not again. After Mr. White tried to kill us, I wanted to disappear. I let you convince me to stay and fight. You said he'd never stop his pursuit. Removing him is the sole path for our safety with Sofia. I believed you because I feared you were correct. My only priority since then has been reuniting with our daughter, while you're lusting for blood. The Taken are not my children, they're my fellow man. What we have done isn't acceptable, and you know it."

He chuckled. "I have loved you from childhood to adulthood. Most of my decisions have been for you or our child. Tú eres mi corazón. I've done everything possible to be the husband you need. In that lifestyle, I neglected my true nature. The extremists awakened the authentic me from slumber. I have done this for you and the rest of the affected individuals. What's wrong with a little self-indulgence?"

She pointed to the blue Reapers, red Thinkers, and yellow Hunters around the room. "This isn't self-indulgence. It's something else."

Mateo tapped himself in the chest with his right index finger. "I acted, even if you think I moved the wrong way with my decisions. Mr. White will never stop looking for us after my actions. So letting my bloodlust out is our best opportunity for longevity. After killing those men in my adolescence, I have embraced it. Why don't you? I'm not the only killer here."

Her eyes moistened.

He pointed at her. "Do you deny the fact that you and I are alike? You've ended lives before, and you'll end them again. It's only a matter of time."

Andrea walked over to Mateo. She looked at him as tears ran down her cheeks and slapped him. Mateo grabbed his face and chuckled.

She stared at him. "Yes, I took someone's life. He'd killed my parents and murdered my sister after he raped her. I entered my house that day and saw my family dead too. A man's laughter came from upstairs. I crept up the steps and held a gaze with my sibling as she took her last breaths."

Andrea wiped the tears from her cheeks. "I'd just missed the chance to save her. Quickly, I grabbed scissors and lunged at him in surprise. I drove them into his neck until he collapsed. My arrival was too late. I tried to revive her, but I couldn't. Then you showed up after avenging your parents."

She was silent for a moment. "So, I have taken a soul. That was the worst thing I've ever done, and I wish it never occurred. It didn't bring my loved ones back. In that moment, knowing he had murdered three members of my household, I understood he wouldn't hesitate to slay me. So, I killed him first to save my life."

Andrea paused. "But you were already aware of my feelings about that. You've known the story since it happened. Mateo, you're aware of my strong disdain for that day, that event. We haven't spoken of it in years and yet, you now throw it in my face to justify what you've become. I may not be one hundred percent human anymore, but you are the biggest monster here."

Mateo clapped. "Finally, you unleash the rage. That anger will guide you down the path it has shown me. Committing the second murder is easier. You would've realized that if you'd aimed at Oliver instead of to his left. He tried to kill us too."

She shook her head. "I wasn't aiming for him. When bullets hit our HoverCopter, I lost focus. I'm not like you."

Andrea held her hand out. "Look around you. A species that you've unleashed on innocents encircles the room. Therefore, he did that. It's his job to stop threats. That is what we are. Our actions resulted in more harm. They put Sofia in danger. Even though he tried to do his duties, that doesn't mean I would hurt someone who used to be our friend."

He scoffed. "Oliver stopped being my friend a long time ago. He determined his role in my world with his deeds."

Mateo glanced about and slammed his fist. "We are wasting minutes. If they didn't damage our aircraft, we'd have left the city to do this. Mr. White has checkpoints on the streets with agents stationed there. We're being sought by HoverCopters and sky drones. I need the Evolution formula, but making it requires time."

She pointed at both of them. "We should just leave. Locate Sofia and vanish to reunite as a family. Is this formula worth your life?"

He nodded. "Without it, the last phase of my plan won't happen."

Mateo banged his hand on the desk three more times. "Had you paid better attention to our daughter, we would have Evolution in our hands instead of trying to recreate it."

Andrea narrowed her gaze. "Forget that formula. Had you cared more about our child, we would have her and be gone."

She closed her eyes and sighed. "I have loved you for decades, but I want our old life back. Before the bombing and the Taken. When we had happiness, and our daughter. I love Sofia, and I yearn for her to be with me once more. Letting her go with them was a mistake, influenced by you and that man."

He waved Andrea away. "I made the right decision, and I'd do it one hundred more times."

Andrea motioned to herself. "What about me? Would you trade me for the formula without delay if you could?"

Mateo paused. He looked at the tear rolling down her face.

He cleared his throat. "Yes."

She started crying.

Mateo held his head a little higher. "Every choice I have made since we escaped Colombia has been with you or Sofia in mind. Every single decision. This one choice is for me, and I won't change my stance."

Andrea studied his expression. "Who are you?"

She walked around him towards the door.

He raised his voice. "Where are you going?"

Andrea turned. "To get air, and to distance myself from you."

She sighed and pivoted back towards the exit. "What do you care? Don't you have a formula to recreate?"

Mateo sucked his teeth three times. "I never said I didn't care. Mr. White is looking for us with all his agents and tech. You shouldn't be out at night. Your luminescence will be easy to spot."

Andrea punched through the doorframe. "I won't go outside, but I am not staying in this lab with a stranger."

She turned and marched out. Mateo stood there for a few minutes. He observed the hole in the door frame. A range of emotions ran through his mind. He exhaled and returned to his HoloPad.

Chapter Five

L iam drove them down the snow-covered Highway Eighty-Two towards Downtown Allegheny. The powdery snowflakes dispersed to the sides from underneath the HoverVan's thrusters and danced in the wind behind it. Hills stretched on the right side of the road. The frozen river lay on the left. Warm air blew through the vents and heated the car to fight the cold. Robert occupied the passenger seat. James sat behind Liam, rubbing Sofia's right arm as she leaned her head on his shoulder and laid her hand on his chest.

He kissed her forehead. "What happens after we finish this?"

She rose and looked at him. "We pretend it never happened. I want everything to be normal again. The way they were, but with you in my updated every day."

James smiled at her.

Sofia grinned back. "I see us waking up beside each other, sharing a meal, and beginning our day. Robert can ride to school with us, and I'll drop you off at your work before returning home to work on my business."

She looked toward the roof of the van. "We'll coordinate our lunch breaks and call each other. I'll go to the coffee shop and get us drinks and snacks that we'll enjoy when I pick you up from work. We'd return to our place and make dinner. Then relax with wine and entertainment afterwards."

James nodded. "That sounds amazing to me. Glad you signed me up for it."

They both chuckled.

He sighed. "I wish I had spoken sooner. It was a lengthy process to move on from losing Jess. The idea of never seeing her again was something I couldn't accept. I could not do it when I tried."

James looked at her. "After some time, I accepted I had to live without her. A week later, I went to a building mixer and met a certain someone."

He smiled. "You stole my breath from across the room the moment I first saw you. I knew I had to meet you. By midnight I was hooked. I also felt conflicted and scared. It had been nine months since the bombing, and a sense of guilt overwhelmed me as I contemplated being with someone else."

James paused. "We were together for two years. I was uncertain about starting a different relationship, but I wanted to be yours. Whenever I caught sight of you at mixers or in the lobby, I started conversations, but I hesitated as I went back and forth. I attempted to be charming, but not too forward. Then yesterday occurred, and this happened."

They exchanged smiles.

He rubbed her arm. "Hearing you describe your vision for us, it's what I want. That's the partnership I need. I'm glad we both think alike."

Sofia grinned. "A few months ago, I planned to talk about our situation. I was living in my parents' home when they attacked. When they hadn't returned, being alone in that house was hard. I saw them daily, my whole life. To not have them was too much. After the incident, I left their place and moved in with my best friend Lydia and her boyfriend. She helped me deal with losing my parents. Without her, that would've been a harder process. Three months ago, we moved to our complex in separate apartments. I decided to give them space. Lydia and I still spent ample time together. We planned on celebrating me quitting yesterday."

She frowned, and James pulled her closer.

Sofia cleared her throat. "When I first arrived, I figured I should meet the new neighbors. I joined Lydia and her boyfriend at the mixer, but they were arguing and left early. Their absence made me feel uneasy. I didn't start conversations with anyone. They never approached me either. Then you walked towards me and saved me from the awkwardness. From the start, I found you attractive and felt a strong connection."

She grabbed his hand. "When we spoke afterwards, I sensed you had feelings for me. I tried to send you signals, but it seemed like you were holding yourself back. Now I know why. I was in no rush to find somebody else."

Sofia looked deep into his eyes. "You and I had a connection, and I wanted to find out where our conversations went. At the army base, I realized waiting for you to make a move was the wrong call. I wasted time by not asking you out. This situation showed me we need to be present."

James leaned in and kissed her.

He pulled his lips from hers and smiled. "Then let us enjoy every moment as if it's our last."

She grinned. "Who said that?"

James shrugged. "Me, just now."

They chuckled together.

He smirked at her. "Regardless, that's a great relationship credo."

Sofia nodded. She resumed leaning her head on his shoulder and laid her hand on his chest.

James rubbed her right arm and beamed. *'This is what I needed.'* he thought.

Chapter Six

Colonel Brian knocked on one of the tall oak double doors. Nobody responded inside the house. He pounded against the wood on his second try, and they detected muffled voices on the other side. General Johnson kicked down one door with his cybernetic leg. It crashed onto the white marble floor in the main hallway. A gold and crystal chandelier blew in the frigid wind as snow swirled within the residence. Past the white columns to the left lay the living room. Flames smoldered in the fireplace. An older man in his sixties jumped up and grabbed a fire poker. His wife pulled their seven-year-old son closer under the comforter on the sofa. He placed his slim frame between the General and his family. General Johnson entered. Blue lights on his cybernetic arm illuminated the area. Colonel Brian, Isaac, and a dozen agents filed in behind him. Another twelve agents stood guard outside the property.

The man held up a cautionary hand. "Who are you? What do you want?"

The General smiled. "I'm General Oliver Johnson. Nice to meet you, Dr. Jesper. This must be Mrs. Jesper and your son, Adam. Have you spotted any odd creatures around here after explosions in the sky yesterday?"

Dr. Jesper nodded. "Yes, hence why we are under comforters and not using our fireplace anymore. We can't use our heat since the power is out. When the blue monsters passed through yesterday, we stayed silent, and they kept going. More came through later. This time, they had a red monster with them. It saw the flames burning in our neighbor's hearth down the street and sent the blue ones into their house."

He gazed through the window. "As I extinguished the fire, we heard the screams of our friends. After that, it was quiet. The monsters continued walking. They stopped right in front of our home. As I peeked, the red creature glanced in this direction for a moment. I thought it saw me, but they kept going. Another fire was not a choice. I didn't want what happened to our neighbors to happen to us."

General Johnson walked over to the mantle. "Was there anybody with them?"

The doctor scratched his head. "You mean like a human?"

The General nodded.

Dr. Jesper shook his head. "No. Who would dare join a group of monsters?"

General Johnson lifted a photo from the Jesper's fireplace. "These two."

He handed the physician the photo.

Dr. Jesper raised his eyes. "They have been dead for a year."

The General raised his cybernetic arm. "Let me assure you they're very much alive. I would recognize my old friends anywhere. Especially when one of them did this to me."

The doctor inspected his left limbs. "Mateo did this to you?"

General Johnson shook his head. "Andrea blew off my left arm and leg."

Dr. Jesper's jaw dropped. "She did that? How in the world?"

The General pointed to the picture. "This version of her does not exist anymore. She is now part Taken. A genetically enhanced mutant, only she also has psychokinetic abilities. It's possible I tried to blow her up with the missile that did this to me."

General Johnson cleared his throat. "That's unimportant. The fact that Mateo, Andrea, and a bunch of Taken were here is important."

The General walked in circles around Dr. Jesper. "I enjoyed your story about your neighbors dying and your fear, but you're lying to me."

General Johnson smiled at him. "You omitted that you're a licensed HoverCopter pilot. That would explain why the one we shot down crashed close to here. So why don't you tell me their destination?"

The doctor shook his head. "I've told you; they died in the bombings last year. We haven't seen them since before that day."

The General sucked his teeth. "I hate it when people lie to me. Tell me the truth, or I will break you. I have broken men way stronger than you. So, I'm going to ask you one more time. What do you know?"

Dr. Jesper glanced at his wife and child. "I'm telling you the truth. I haven't laid eyes on them in over a year."

General Johnson sighed. "Okay."

He patted the doctor on the shoulder with his cybernetic arm with a smile on his face.

The General looked to his agents. "Tear this place apart until you find a clue about their location."

The agents searched through drawers and cabinets. They ascended to the top floors and descended to the basement. General Johnson moved towards Mrs. Jesper.

Dr. Jesper jumped between them. "Stay away from my family."

General Johnson chuckled. "Get out of my way, for your own good."

He walked around Dr. Jesper. The fire poker bounced off the General's cybernetic arm. The doctor took one step back as agents all focused on him. General Johnson slowly turned. As Dr. Jesper apologized, General Johnson's cybernetic arm lifted him into the air by his throat. He tried to pry at General Johnson's fingers, to no avail. Their son Adam cried.

Isaac's eyes widened. '*What is he doing*?!' he thought.

Mrs. Jesper shielded her child. "Please, stop hurting my husband!"

The General eyed her. "I'll quit as soon as one of you tell me the details I need."

Mrs. Jesper shook her head. "We know nothing."

General Johnson gave her a smile. "I think otherwise."

He increased his grip. Mrs. Jesper and her son continued to scream.

Isaac stepped up to the General. "That's enough. We can find them another way. Don't do this. Especially in front of his family."

General Johnson looked at Mrs. Jesper. "He brought this upon himself. I offered him the easier path twice. Your husband chose the hard road when he attacked me. Since time isn't a luxury we have, I reward his attack beyond the ramifications he envisioned."

Dr. Jesper started going limp.

Mrs. Jesper jumped to her feet. "Alright, I'll tell you. Just don't kill him."

The General dropped Dr. Jesper. "Start talking."

Mrs. Jesper moved towards her spouse, who was gasping for breath.

General Johnson waved his cybernetic finger from side to side. "You stay there until you share the information I want, or he goes back in the air."

Mrs. Jesper nodded. "They were here after they crashed. Those monsters followed them. Mateo tried to recruit him to help recreate a formula. My husband almost died in that HoverCopter crash, so I told him no. Mateo threatened the neighborhood. Andrea attempted to dissuade him from it. Something was wrong with her. She didn't look normal, her skin... glowed. I informed Mateo he wasn't leaving a second time. He smiled and left. When they were outside, we heard them arguing. That's when Mateo kept his word. He sent his creatures to all our neighbors' homes. We watched through the window as screaming came from all around us. Then everything was silent."

Tears fell down her face. "More creatures emerged than entered. Mateo pointed at their houses and screamed that the entire neighborhood had died because of our choice."

She shook her head. "He's right. We could've saved our friends, but we didn't think he'd hurt them. He said that they wouldn't spare our house again."

Tears fell from Mrs. Jesper's eyes. "The Mateo we knew was gentle, loving, and caring. His experiences in the past year, whatever they may be, have broken him."

The General took a step closer. "The formula he asked your husband to help with may be the best chance we have to stop him and Andrea before this city is beyond saving. He made it for our boss. After a little misunderstanding, he turned against our agency. My employer needs that formula to save us all."

General Johnson approached and placed his hand on Mrs. Jesper's shoulder. "Your neighbors are now Taken. When his Reapers bite their victim, they become Taken themselves. It's a major threat because of the potential explosion in numbers. So yes, your friends becoming those monsters is your fault. However, there's something you can do to stop the man responsible. Tell me his destination, so we're able to prevent him from doing more damage than he already has."

Mrs. Jesper nodded. "He mentioned the research campus in Downtown. Mateo didn't mention a specific lab or building, but that's where they headed."

The General smiled. "Thank you for your help, Mrs. Jesper. We'll make sure he pays for what he's done to your neighbors."

General Johnson looked at Dr. Jesper and then back to Mrs. Jesper. "Make sure in the future your husband spares himself from painful lessons. The next guy may not be as nice as me."

Mrs. Jesper gave a nod. The General headed for the door and the agents followed him. She and their son ran to Dr. Jesper. They cried as they hugged him. Isaac watched before exiting into the frigid air.

He saw General Johnson conversing with Mr. White through a holographic projection.

Isaac walked over to Colonel Brian. "What the hell was that?"

Brian shook his head. "I'm not sure. I've never seen him act like that. Do you think it's his cybernetics?"

Isaac looked at him. "Maybe. I believe it's more related to the person who hurt him. That's not how you treat civilians. There are better ways to get information."

The General cleared his throat. "Would we have discovered it soon enough to stop them?"

Isaac turned to him. "That's undetermined. We should not be attacking non-combatants. Especially in front of their families. No matter what they knew. An innocent child was present that didn't need to witness that."

General Johnson crossed his arms. "So, tell me how we would have found them quicker?"

Isaac stood there.

The General pointed at him. "You don't know? Do you have any idea who was aware of their whereabouts?"

Isaac's gaze narrowed.

General Johnson gestured over his shoulder. "The adults in that house. So now we're aware which couple of buildings they're in instead of us standing here wondering which of the hundreds of labs in this city they're at now."

Isaac shook his head. "You almost killed him in front of his wife and child."

The General held up a finger. "The key word is almost. I understand how to bring a person to the brink of death. Believe it or not, I agree with you Isaac. We should not treat civilians in that manner. They were not civilians. He's a co-conspirator. Dr. Jesper lied right to my face, multiple times. I tried to be reasonable, as you saw with your own eyes. They should be in handcuffs and headed to The Agency. Lucky for them, our mission was to get information. The safest place in the city is our headquarters. Being left to fend for themselves is their punishment."

General Johnson patted Isaac on the shoulder. "Perhaps field work in The Agency isn't the right fit for you. I've heard remarkable things about you over the years from Brian. Your exploits and skills are familiar to me. It's possible that your best days are behind you. You don't seem to have the nerve to do the hard things. Not everybody does. That's what separates the powerful from the weak. The haves from the have nots. The leaders from the followers. If you fall into any of those latter categories, we'll find you a nice safe desk job to keep you from having to get your hands dirty. Only because you're Brian's friend. We wouldn't want you to end up falling from grace like your father."

Isaac turned to Brian.

Colonel Brian raised his hands and shook his head. "I didn't tell them anything."

The General chuckled. "He did not give me the information. Mr. White told me. He always does his homework on anybody he recruits. Mr. White knows everyone's darkest secrets, including yours."

General Johnson walked up to Isaac as other agents circled. "We lacked time to play games with them, and I don't need to explain myself to you. When we met, you were Brian's best friend. A brother even. So, I treated you like family. I gave you the respect one would give friends of their closest companion. Now you fall under my command. You will show me the respect you owe your commanding officer, or I will send you back to The Agency. We achieved our goal."

Isaac nodded. "Yes, we did, but at what cost? If we're going to be interacting with civilians, we need to prove to them they can trust The Agency. With what you did in that house, I don't trust us. Government should not behave like this."

The General laughed and slapped Isaac on the shoulder. "Who ever said The Agency was part of the government?"

Isaac turned to Brian. "I guess that's what I get for assuming."

General Johnson smiled. "We are above the government. We outrank them and don't have to adhere to any of their protocols thanks to the President. If that makes you uncomfortable, maybe The Agency just isn't for you."

The General walked away.

Isaac looked at the Jesper's house. "Maybe it isn't."

Moments later, more drones joined the ones that hovered above the residence as they sped towards the Allegheny Research Campus.

Chapter Seven

Mr. White sat in his dimly lit office behind a black mahogany desk. The smoke from his previous cigar remained in the air. He still detected the coffee note from his last drag. Mr. White picked up his glass of bourbon and sipped. "That's the information that we have about the four variations of Taken."

Madam President Mary Jackson stood before him via hologram, which provided most of the lighting in the room.

She nodded. "What's the current situation with the power being restored to the city?"

Mr. White swiped his HoloPad and altered the holographic image. "The electric company's crews have been working around the clock to restore electricity. I'm told repairs should finish soon. They had to bring in 6G chips from outside the blast radiuses and change every single one."

He marked parts of the picture. "We've positioned agents in case Mateo targets the power plants again."

Mr. White showed another map. "Half of the Taken gathered in Downtown Allegheny. They went to their creators after their HoverCopter crashed."

President Jackson nodded. "That's a good thing. Eliminating them becomes easier when they gather in one place."

Mr. White shook his head. "Last night, that would've been plausible. Because of the incident at Mateo's lab, their numbers grew exponentially.

We are now talking one hundred thousand Taken in the city. Half are in Downtown Allegheny."

President Jackson frowned. "This is terrible. I'm going to send troops and national guard units from the nearby areas in Keystone, Franklin, and West Dominion."

Mr. White nodded. "Send them, but not into town. Have them reinforce my agents on the perimeter around the county, so nothing or nobody gets out. We need to strategize to prevent this from leaking. That's why power and water are being restored but the internet, cable, and cellular isn't. The E.M.P. fried all 6G chips in devices, so the threat of it getting out on social media is minimal."

The President nodded. "What about those responsible? What info do we have on their current location?"

Mr. White brought up a model of the Allegheny Research Campus. "General Johnson got information from someone they know. We know they're in one of these buildings. Drones are en route to establish a visual. Oliver and his team are also on the way to apprehend them."

President Jackson stood and leaned on her desk. "Are we sure that a cure exists, or that we can trust him to create it?"

Mr. White drank more bourbon. "Men such as Mateo never lack an escape plan for emergencies. As for trusting him, when he demonstrates that I can't rely on him is when I'll kill him myself."

The President resumed seating. "How will you carry out Plan Bravo, and what's the progress?"

Mr. White brought up a map of the area. "As you know, the goal of Plan Alpha was prevention. That operation was unsuccessful. I underestimated Mateo. That won't happen again. Plan Bravo is all about containment."

He zoomed into the image. "Since most of the Taken are in a central location, we'll contain them inside a larger perimeter. Eight squads will sweep a specific direction from five miles outside the boundary to the border itself to make sure no Taken has escaped. Your soldiers and national guardsmen are going to patrol the barrier to double check."

Mr. White stared into her eyes. "If the blockade strategy fails, Plan Charlie and Plan Delta must begin at once. If they escape the city, they'll have the numbers to overtake the world in weeks."

President Jackson shook her head. "Make sure Plan Bravo works. Plan Charlie is a last resort measure. Plan Delta is unproven, and extremely dangerous. The long-term effects of it are unknown to us."

Mr. White nodded. "That's true, but I'll do what's needed to save this city and the Americas. We'll turn to those plans if we must."

The President smiled. "Thank God you are with me. You have always had multiple strategies in mind by the time I'm done explaining situations to you."

Mr. White grinned. "As I recall, this skill of mine got you elected as the first President of the United Continents of America. Well, that and my trade secrets."

She raised her hands. "I know nothing about that."

Mr. White chuckled. "That was by design. You kept yourself untainted, and I ensured a fair election for you. Your Presidency was what we needed in a time of such division. You united us and brought everyone together like no one else could. After World War Three, you saved the continents."

President Jackson smiled. "Without you, I would not have gotten a fair chance to do it."

She chuckled. "We have shared many experiences. Do you recall the time in high school when Shar came out in an inappropriate bathing suit for swimming class? Coach Frank sprinted over with a towel."

They laughed in unison.

Mr. White clapped his hands. "Remember when Scott threw a drink at the French teacher and a puddle of soda formed on top of his head?"

As he chuckled, Mary shook her head. "I can't recall that."

Mr. White scratched his head. "Are you sure? We giggled so much about it, he thought we did it. So, he kicked us out of the classroom, and sent us to the principal."

She shook her head. "I'll take your word for it. You know my memory is spotty. Yours is still impeccable as ever."

He peered away for a moment.

His gaze returned to Mary. "I believe I'm doing what's right. All my decisions were correct when made. Certain choices have shaped the person I've become. I have always tried to assess the situation and make the best judgment. In hindsight, a few decisions were incorrect. I'd change a couple of them if possible. Others I would not. That's the difference between me and the leaders of other agencies. I act, and don't judge myself if it's the wrong choice. If I'm wrong, I move on to the next event. My excellence at work stems from this."

Mr. White took another sip of bourbon and savored it for a moment.

He placed the glass on the desk. "In the past, my decisions have affected a handful of people. Some have protected this city and the continents from outside threats. I never doubted any decision before it had played out until today. Progressing with Plan Charlie and Plan Delta are the first two choices that cause me to hesitate. The lives at stake are countless. The risks from these Taken are unlike anything the world's seen. Plan Charlie is necessary if Plan Bravo doesn't work. Plan Delta must execute as planned or the cost will be dire."

Mr. White clasped his hands together. "Should we continue with these plans or devise an alternative course of action?"

President Jackson shook her head. "You forget, we made these decisions as a team. I know what both phases entail. If we make a mistake, the consequences are severe, but if we succeed, we save many lives. I have considered if we should move forward or find an alternative. We agreed this was the correct choice. We lacked a better method to protect U.C.A. citizens. As I sit here twenty-four hours later, I still do not see a different choice. If one hundred thousand Taken escape the city limits, it threatens the entire globe."

Mr. White analyzed her eyes. '*How much of that's her thoughts versus my words to her*?' he thought.

The President chuckled. "Your conviction has a magnetic effect on people."

She studied his face. "You're right about ninety percent of the time. I'll take those odds every day."

He exhaled. '*I wish this was one hundred percent fool proof.*' he thought.

Mr. White was silent. "What if this is a ten percent moment?"

President Jackson shook her head. "It won't be. I have greater confidence in you than in myself. I'm the world's leader, and you are the most powerful man on the planet. Don't lose sight of your identity, roots, and accomplishments. We can do it. You got this."

Mr. White smiled. "Okay, you've convinced me about myself. Let's hope Plan Bravo works. The last two plans are not ideal and too complicated."

He consumed the rest of his bourbon and slammed down the glass. "I'll update you on the progress. If we must start Plan Charlie, just do what we discussed. It is going to work. I'll take care of Plan Delta."

The President nodded. "We'll talk soon 'Mr. White'."

He shook his head. "I hate it when you call me that. Aren't we friends?"

She gave a nod. "The closest. Unlike you, I intend to stay mostly professional."

President Jackson grinned and ended the conversation. Mr. White sat back and smirked before standing. He adjusted his tie and put on his suit jacket as he exited his office towards his next task.

Chapter Eight

Downtown Allegheny, when viewed from above, resembled a triangle.

Two rivers flanked it on either side, converging at the point to form a third river.

The area featured multiple skyscrapers that housed businesses and apartments.

Their exteriors typically showcased neon lights at ground level and holographic billboards on the upper floors.

Every night, holographic banners ascend into the sky, visible for miles.

The towering structures sat dark tonight, illuminated only by the moonlight as they approached the city center in the HoverVan.

James leaned forward. "How are you holding up Liam?"

Liam sighed. "I'm doing my best for now."

He paused. "Why did my dad lock himself out beyond the gate? He tried to buy us time, but he should've found another way. For me."

James put his hand on Liam's shoulder.

Liam exhaled heavily. "Even though I annoyed him a lot, I love my dad. It's our dynamic. I don't want anything to happen to him. I'm unprepared to be without my father."

James nodded. "Losing people is tough. After Jess died last year, I was a wreck for nine months."

He paused. "We'll never understand what went through his mind at that moment, but I'm certain he made what he thought was the best decision. I hope your dad is okay. There's still a chance he survived. If he didn't, then he perished as he lived. A hero through and through."

Liam smiled. "You're like the best friend I never had. That's what I needed. Are you sure you aren't a motivational speaker?"

James nodded. "I am positive. At work, I listened to eight hours of podcasts. I internalized a lot of it and changed my story, which transformed my life."

Liam chuckled. "You need a career change. I'm seeing clearer thanks to you."

They both laughed.

Liam looked at Sofia through the rearview. "Any idea where your dad would go?"

Sofia leaned forward. "My best guess is since we have his life's work, he may try to make more."

Liam nodded. "Where could he go to do that?"

Sofia chuckled. "If I had to pick, it would be The Allegheny Research Campus."

He gave a nod. "Why choose that place over another lab?"

Sofia laughed. "The whole place is basically his. Plus, it has everything he needs for his work. He has access and carte blanche from the people who run it. Many researchers traveled globally just to walk by him once. My dad's famous in the science community because he's the best globally at what he does."

Liam turned to James. "I bet scientists party hard. They probably throw ragers."

Everyone chuckled.

Liam cleared his throat. "What if you're wrong?"

Sofia shrugged. "Then I'm wrong, and we continue to look through the other labs in Downtown Allegheny."

Liam nodded. "How many labs are there in town?"

Sofia counted her fingers. "Let's see. One, two... one hundred fourteen."

Liam blinked his eyes rapidly.

He turned to James. "Sofia better be right. That's too much walking for my tootsies."

James chuckled. "You call your toes tootsies?"

Liam glanced around as everybody laughed. "Doesn't everyone?"

James shook his head. "No, they do not."

Liam looked at Robert. "Come on Rob. All the kids say tootsies, don't they?"

Robert laughed. "Saying that in school would embarrass me so much, I'd quit by second period."

Liam nodded. "I strike tootsies from the vocabulary."

As they exited Highway Eighty-Two towards Downtown Allegheny, Liam slammed on the brakes. The powerful gust of air threw snow in front of them. He parked the HoverVan and shut off the lights.

Liam looked at James and Sofia. "We may have a problem."

He pointed out the windshield. "Agency HoverCars are blocking this road into town."

James shook his head. "How are their cars working when the E.M.P. fried all the others?"

Liam motioned to the left. "I'm not sure, but they're blocking every entrance along the street up to the Shopping District. Every other intersection has two agents armed with weapons."

Robert gestured towards the sky. "There are giant drones up there."

James pointed. "Look at those trucks."

Dozens of HoverFlatbeds passed by them, leaving town. "They're hauling huge construction materials. Agency HoverCars are escorting them."

Sofia faced him. "What would they build right now?"

Liam shook his head. "With Mr. White involved, it's definitely not good news for anyone."

A light shone on them.

Robert looked at James. "They see us. What do we do?"

James met eyes with Liam, who nodded and slipped the car into gear.

One agent pulsed his flashlight at the HoverVan as he put his hand on his holster. "This area's restricted. Please return to your homes for your safety."

Liam floored the gas as he switched on the headlights. The agents ran to their vehicles. Liam accelerated to the left, down the boulevard that stretched along the west river's side of town. As they got to the next intersection, he turned right into the vacant alley.

Sofia pointed. "Pull over and follow me."

Liam stopped the van, and everyone hopped out. Sofia led them as they sprinted across the street. She pulled out a key and opened one of the double doors of a convenience store. Sofia locked the door after them. They took cover behind the shelves at the end of the aisles as multiple cars parked a block away where they ditched the HoverVan.

An agent shouted. "Find them, now. If it's Liam Smith and the other civilians, do not shoot."

Liam shook his head. "I knew they would seek us out."

Robert looked at him. "Why would he be looking for us?"

James sighed. "It can't be the formula. I don't think they know we had it."

Sofia turned to James. "He'll be mad when he finds out we drank it."

Liam shushed them. He pointed to the front window. Two sources of light were growing closer. A pair of agents arrived at the door and tried to open it. They shone their flashlights through the glass. James heard a howl. The lights ceased shining inside the store. Liam peeked out at the operatives. They went left of the shop.

An agent yelled. "Shoot! Shoot them now!"

Both individuals opened fire. Something quickly overtook them. They listened to flesh tearing below the window. Robert covered his ears. The sound of eating halted. One creature slammed up against the front door.

Liam returned to cover. "Shit. It spotted me."

James pointed towards the entrance. "What saw you? Was that what we heard at Lemon Station?"

Liam shook his head. "I don't know, but it's not Taken. It looked like a human, but with desaturated skin. Its eyes glowed white."

Liam rotated into a kneel, aiming at the front. James and Sofia did the same.

James turned to Robert. "Get ready."

Robert breathed heavier. Shots came from the right side of the building. The creatures roared. They sprinted at their attackers. A bullet shattered the top pane of the right door. It shattered the front window on the left wall. One of the agents outside gasped for air as he laid on the sidewalk. A door banged open behind them.

A man emerged, brandishing a pistol. "Get the hell out before I..."

He stopped and stared at Sofia. "You've got nerve."

She sighed. "Hey Roger."

Chapter Nine

They stood in the dark store, at the end of the aisles towards the backroom. Roger pointed his pistol at Sofia from a few feet away. James stepped in front of her, Liam walked to his right, and Robert moved to his left.

Liam held his hand up and slowly pulled his badge from his back right pocket. "My name is Captain Liam Smith, and I need you to put down your weapon."

Roger shook his head. "I'm not putting shit down until she leaves my store."

Liam chuckled.

He turned to James. "Did I say it in Spanish?"

James stared at Roger. "No, you didn't."

Liam pinched the bridge of his nose. "Listen sunshine, that wasn't a request. That was more of a command. So, keep aiming at her, and see what happens next."

Roger gritted his teeth and handed the pistol to Liam. "Alright, you have my weapon."

Liam checked the magazine and the chamber. "Good, because I didn't have one."

Roger shook his head. "What kind of cop are you?"

Liam smiled. "The best, of course."

Sofia stepped between James and Liam.

She cleared her throat. "I'm not sorry for what I did yesterday, but you had it coming. I told you if you kept harassing me, I would knock you unconscious. You slapped my ass, and I left you laying there. Can we move on like adults?"

"Hell no." Roger took a step closer to Sofia. "The punks who were here at the time saw me unresponsive. They stole money and products."

He grabbed his jaw. "I woke up in complete darkness because the power is out everywhere. When I went to leave, my HoverCar wouldn't start. My HoloWatch stopped working, so I wasn't able to get a ride home through the Shofer app. I had no choice but to stay here, unless I wanted to walk to Robertson Township."

Roger pointed outside. "Now men in black suits have Downtown surrounded, and there're all kinds of monsters running around killing everything that moves out there. I would've been at my place barricaded inside in comfort if you hadn't attacked me."

He pressed his finger into her shoulder and pushed.

James moved from behind Sofia on the left and shoved Roger back. "Touch her again and see what happens."

Liam stepped up and positioned himself beside James on the right. "Ditto."

Robert walked next to his dad.

Sofia switched places with them once more. "Thanks, guys, but I got this."

They stood aside.

She clapped her hands together. "So, are you mad about the punch, or about me not wanting you? Either way, this isn't the time."

Roger chuckled. "I thought you would appreciate a guy who navigated from the Lower District by himself. But you're just another bougie Middle District bitch."

She laughed softly. On her left, James stared at Roger, and Robert shook his head. On her right, Liam turned to the shelf beside him, opened a bag of popcorn, and threw a handful at his mouth.

She smiled at Roger. Then she kicked him in the balls.

He fell to the floor.

She dusted her hands. "I respect someone like that, but not when they act superior to everyone. People don't dislike you because of where you lived. They hate you because you're an ass."

Sofia kneeled next to Roger. "And for your information, I'm from the Upper District."

He struggled to his feet. Liam aimed the pistol in the air. Roger took a step toward Sofia. James and Robert stepped in front of her. Liam unleashed a shot into the ceiling. Plaster, wood, and a light fell to the ground.

Roger grabbed his head. "That's my roof."

Liam directed his aim at him. "Next time, it will be your head. Look, I already have her saying you slapped her ass. Sexual assault, harassment allegations, and your forceful poke. I should arrest you. Since we have way more important things to do than deal with you, you're getting off easy. Come on everybody, let's..."

He froze at the sight of two women emerging from the backroom.

Liam smiled. "Emily?"

Emily was a thirty-four-year-old with warm ivory skin, and green eyes with brown around the pupil. She stood five feet eight inches tall, with long brunette hair, and a thin frame. She wore a blue peacoat with a white shirt underneath and light blue jeans. Emily ran to Liam, and they hugged each other.

He held her shoulders at arm's length. "Where did you vanish to last year?"

Emily sighed. "That's a complicated story."

They grinned at each other. Sofia stepped to James' right, smiling. She turned to him, but he didn't see Liam's reunion with Emily. His gaze fixated on the other woman. James' eyes widened and watered while his jaw dropped.

The woman was crying. She stood five feet six inches tall with golden-brown skin, light brown almond-shaped eyes, and a mane of curly black hair. The woman wore a purple hoodie with dark blue jeans. She ran at James and threw herself into his arms, grabbed his face, and kissed him. He embraced her. Sofia stepped to the right.

James' breathing increased. "I thought you were dead."

With tears streaming down his face, Robert ran to her and embraced her tightly.

James turned to Sofia. "Sofia, this is Jess."

Chapter Ten

In the back of Roger's dark and chilly convenience store in Downtown Allegheny, James pinched himself. '*I must be dreaming*.' he thought.

Jess chuckled. "I've missed you so much Jamie."

James stared at her. "I thought you were dead."

She shook her head. "I believed I would be too."

He touched her face. "What happened?"

Jess held his hand against her cheek. "We went to The Outlets Downtown. I needed to get some items for our honeymoon. Desaray, Whitney, Tasha, and I were at Lemon Station when the attack happened. There was an explosion outside just as we boarded the train. It spewed these yellow particles into the building. After that, the scene was chaotic."

James shook his head. "So, the bombings exposed you to Remnant."

She nodded. "Is that what it's called? Anyway, we all were. I guess it triggered a lockdown when it detected the explosion or the Remnant. The station sealed itself."

Jess shook her head. "We had no way to get out. Not through the doors or the tracks. I tried calling you, but my HoloWatch wasn't working. Tasha called the police, but her call didn't go through either."

He frowned. "Maybe the security measure blocked the phone signals."

She nodded. "Everyone panicked. The crowd screamed and ran. The injured cried for help. We tried to help them. People were dead all around the station. Within moments, those exposed to the substance got sick. Including Desaray and Whitney."

James squeezed her hand. "How long did it take?"

Jess frowned. "About five minutes. They coughed at first. Then they had fevers."

She sniffled. "After that, they writhed on the floor in pain. Tasha and I tried to help, but we didn't know how. Within half an hour, they were all dead."

Tears poured from her eyes. "Everybody in the station had perished except for a married couple, me, and Tasha. We all cried. They'd lost children. Two of my friends died. Tasha's friend and sister were gone."

He wiped her tears away. "I'm so sorry about Desi and Whit."

Jess nodded as she frowned.

She exhaled. "About an hour after the explosion, the tunnels opened, and another train arrived. A couple dozen people in full hazmat suits stepped off and inspected the scene. Four of them approached us and asked questions."

James rubbed her hand with his thumb. "What did they ask?"

Jess smiled at his touch. "They requested identification. Then they examined us before leading everyone onto the other train. They called them negative pressure cars. They put Tasha and me in one car, while the couple occupied the other car. I asked to call you. They said I'd be able to after the testing was done. First, they wanted to make sure the substance wasn't contagious or dangerous. As we rode, she cried on my shoulder. When we got there, they separated us from the married husband and wife again."

His brows furrowed. "Why did they divide you into pairs?"

She shook her head. "I don't know. They never explained why they did it. The doctors did a lot of tests after our arrival. Every time we requested to contact our families, they assured us we would soon. They kept taking more blood for testing. Allegedly, they found complications in our results, and they needed to be sure we wouldn't endanger our loved ones, or the public. After months of exams, they stated we seemed to be immune to the chemicals."

Her eyebrows furrowed. "I asked about the husband and wife. We hadn't seen them since we arrived. Apparently, they were immune at first. It turned out they were only resistant."

Jess rubbed her knee. "They were slowly succumbing to the chemical. I cooperated as much as possible. So I could tell you I was alive and returning to you."

She wiped away a tear. "Tasha was done cooperating. Two days ago, they came to get blood, and she fought them. She knocked one guard unconscious. They dragged her from the room. I tried to stop them from taking her, but two of the nurses restrained me."

James examined her. "Did they hurt you?"

Jess shook her head. "No, they didn't harm me. Tasha wouldn't talk after they returned her. She sat up, holding her legs close, and rocked. I asked what happened, but Tasha paid no attention to me. When the power shut off last night, the call bell stopped working. We stayed silent for a few minutes. Then we heard the doctors and nurses screaming down the hall. The screams snapped Tasha out of her daze. There were no door handles. The doors locked from the outside. Without electricity, the door required manual unlocking."

He placed his hand on her knee. "How did you get out?"

"A doctor opened it and told us to run. I grabbed her hand, and we ran. A creature attacked the doctor when we exited." she said.

Jess paused. "I wanted to help, but we needed to survive. This was the first opportunity for us to escape the medical prison where we had been detained for a year. As we neared the exit, dead guards, doctors, and nurses were all around the lobby. A guard turned with his gun raised. Our arrival startled him, and he shot in our direction. I asked what the hell was wrong with him, but he ignored me. He stared at Tasha."

She looked at the sky. "The guard shot her in the stomach. Tasha fell to her knees while she gazed at me. Fear filled her eyes. At that moment, everything surrounding us disappeared. I forgot I was in danger. Tasha was all that was important. I clenched her hand and begged her to fight. We cried together until she died."

James rubbed her hand with his thumb. "I'm so sorry."

Jess took a deep breath. "I didn't notice the guard approach. When I saw him hovering over us, I got to my feet and shoved him as hard as possible. As he stumbled back, another monster pounced on him. It wore the same patient clothing as Tasha and me. The creature that attacked him was the married woman, except her skin was pale and her eyes were glowing white. Only then did I realize it was her husband that tackled the doctor outside our room. He screamed as she fed, and I felt no pity for him. The wife paused for a second and gazed at me. The guard's blood covered her mouth. That returned the fear to me. She refrained from attacking me. The wife just glanced at me before feeding again. When I left the building, I spotted the hospital, Allegheny University, and the stadium."

He shook his head. "You were in Uptown Allegheny this whole time?"

She nodded. "Wearing a patient gown, I sprinted towards Downtown through the snow in socks. I was freezing, but I kept going. Survival motivated me, as did you."

Jess touched James' face. "Thank God I bumped into her over there. Emily stood outside the bar where she worked. Emily talked about the power outage to employees from the surrounding businesses. I dashed up to them and asked for help. She led me indoors. We made our way to her apartment above her job, using the back steps. Emily warmed me up and gave me clothes, boots, food, and drink. I told her everything that happened. As I finished, we heard screams. We went to the window. A group of the pale creatures were near the building."

His eyes widened. "Like the husband and wife?"

She nodded. "Yeah, but there were more creatures in the street. The spouses weren't among them. They were biting the necks of most of her friends. One of her friends entered the door downstairs. We heard him running up the steps towards her apartment. Something was behind him. A creature howled. I hid under the bed and pulled at her leg. Emily resisted at first, but joined me. The man ran into the bedroom. He stood there for a second, looking for Emily. The monster dragged him to the ground by his neck. His feet were closest to us. Her friend tried to get out of its grip but was unable. After it fed on him, it left. We emerged after we didn't hear it for a few minutes. I covered Emily's mouth when she saw her friend lying dead in front of her. Glancing out the window, I saw no creatures outside. Then another friend of hers turned pale. I called her to look. The man started convulsing. I told her we needed to leave before more of them transformed. Emily and I exited out the rear. We avoided them until we bumped into Roger at the entrance smoking and convinced him to lock the doors once were inside the store. Since yesterday, we've been hiding in the back, trying to stay hidden."

Jess pulled James close. "Thank God I found you. Thinking of you kept me going for the last year."

James cried uncontrollably into her shoulder. "I thought you were dead. It took me nine months to mourn you. I've missed you so much."

She wiped away his tears. "It's okay. I'm here now. We'll savor each moment to make up for lost time."

He looked at Sofia. Jess glanced at her as well.

She smiled at him. "Is she a friend of yours?"

James grabbed her hand. "The last twenty-four hours have been crazy. There's a lot I have to tell you."

Chapter Eleven

The frigid air blew in through the side window the bullet shattered. Liam and Emily stood near the left wall in the dark store. He stared at her. She smiled at him. "Did you miss me?"

Liam nodded. "Of course I did. I still don't understand why you ghosted me though. You're my best friend, and you went away without saying goodbye. I couldn't reach you, and you never let me know you were alright. I take little personal, but the way you left hurt. Because you're tougher than me, I felt you would be fine. My mind would have been at ease if I was sure you were good. I would've told people I was okay before leaving town."

Emily looked at the floor. "I regret not answering or reaching out to you. I knew if we talked, I would come back before I was ready."

He grabbed her hand. "Is that a terrible thing?"

She shook her head. "Not about you. If I had returned home earlier, I wouldn't have been prepared to confront my dad."

Emily sighed. "You're right. I am tougher than you, but my father has us both beat."

Liam rubbed the back of her fingers with his thumb. "Why do you have to confront him?"

She exhaled. "Life was simple being a Colonel's daughter. My dad and I had no issues or arguments. Everything was fine until two years ago. He left for a mission. Nothing unusual."

Emily looked at him. "He traveled in and out of town often. When he returned, something was wrong. He had a temper and picked fights with me for no reason. Afterwards, he'd say sorry, but I never faced that situation before."

He nodded. "I never saw Brian mad at anybody. Annoyed with me sometimes? Yes, but never angry."

She shook her head. "I would discover him crying when he thought I wasn't home. Sometimes I would catch him staring into nothingness. It would take a few minutes to bring him back to reality. Other times, he'd disappear all day and return after midnight. He wouldn't answer any of my messages. I set up a session for him to speak with someone, but he refused to go. The worst part of the change was his growing paranoia."

Emily sighed. "When he missed the therapy appointment, I had to get away. My friends and I visited Silver City for a week. That vacation was what I needed. When I came back home, he drew his gun on me."

She cried. "I froze as we stared at each other. Tears came out of my eyes. He never lowered the pistol, as if he didn't recognize me. It may sound insane, but I believe he would have shot me if I stayed. I backed out of the house and ran."

Liam's eyes widened. "Do you think he would've pulled the trigger?"

Emily nodded. "Yes, but I could've done more to help my dad. I should've tried harder to figure out what was going on with him. When I stopped running, I didn't know what to do. I planned to reach out to you, but you were traveling. My next thought was your father. If anyone would get through to him, it'd be Isaac. With my father in that state, though, I hesitated to send your dad over there. If something happened to him, you'd hate me, and I'd never forgive myself. So, I moved to Silver City. I found a crappy apartment in the Lower District and took bartending classes. Once I met the income requirements for a Middle District residence, I moved to a way nicer place. A month ago, I hit my savings goal. I returned because living in the Middle District here is cheaper."

He crossed his arms. "Is that the only reason?"

She chuckled. "Plus, I missed you. I should've run to you and not ran away. It was a mistake to ignore your calls and not call you back. When I got back a few weeks ago, I was going to surprise you. I was too nervous. People's perception can change with time and space. Thoughts evolve, as do feelings."

Liam chuckled. "What does that mean?"

Emily leaned in and kissed his cheek.

They smiled at each other. "I've wanted to take our relationship to the next level, but always stopped myself. Because we grew up together, and we're friends. I would tell myself it would be too awkward. Then I would date the wrong guys and run to you for comfort. You always consoled me, saying I was too good for them. In those moments, I felt comforted and loved."

She sighed. "It's time to stop running. From my feelings for you, and from my father. As soon as they restore the power, I'm reaching out to him to ask what was happening, and to apologize for leaving."

He frowned.

Emily's smile faded away. "What's wrong Liam?"

Liam exhaled. "After the Taken were unleashed yesterday, I ran into James, Sofia, and Robert. My dad and your father joined us at our station. We traveled to an army base to meet your dad's General. Then we ended up meeting his boss. A guy named Mr. White. We went on a mission to capture the people responsible for creating those mutants. When we breached their lab, they killed Brian."

She covered her mouth and shook her head. "No. It can't be true. He must be alive."

Tears fell down her face. Liam pulled her closer. She cried on his shoulder.

He sighed. "After that, my dad sacrificed himself, so we'd be able to finish the mission. We didn't capture the bad guys, but we stole their life's work. That bought us time. They'll probably attempt to create more at the nearby research campus. We're on our way there now to apprehend them."

Emily wiped away her tears. "Then I'll join you."

Liam looked into her eyes. "This will be dangerous. We are unsure how many Taken we'll have to fight. These pale creatures are still a mystery. We have to beat Mr. White and The Agency there. He's not a fan of me. Are you sure you want to go?"

She nodded. "I'm going."

He smiled at her. "Okay then."

Liam hugged her and rubbed her back. Sofia walked by them. He saw her crying.

Liam turned to Emily. "Would you excuse me for a moment?"

Emily gave a nod. He stood up and went after her.

Chapter Twelve

Sofia stood behind the red counter in the front left corner of the store and watched Jessica and James talk. She tried to listen to what they were saying, but Liam and Emily were discussing something closer to where she was located. Robert walked over and positioned himself beside Sofia.

They both examined his father's conversation. Robert had a slight smile, while she had a faint frown. Both expressions disappeared when their eyes met one another. Sofia nodded towards James and Jessica. "I bet this situation is crazy for you."

He gave a nod. "Yeah. We were told she died. I took it hard. It was harder on my dad. Jess was special to both of us."

Robert looked at his father and Jessica. "She never tried to be my mom or replace her. Jess was just my friend. He was sad for months after the attack. When he met you, he got back to normal. It's been great to have him be his old self again."

Sofia smiled. "I'm glad he returned to being himself for you."

She stared at James and Jessica. "Tell me something. How long were they together before everything happened?"

He looked up. "About four years."

Her slight frown resurfaced. '*How do I compete with that*?' she thought.

Sofia turned to Robert. "So, how is she as a person?"

He beamed. "She's so funny. Jess would make us breakfast on the weekends and cook dinner every other night. We'd all watch sports together. She would always reward me with games when I got good grades in school."

Robert grinned. "Jess is awesome."

He hid his smile once he saw Sofia's expression. "You're amazing too."

She pretended to grin in response.

Sofia hugged Robert. "You're pretty incredible yourself."

She stood and walked to the rear hallway near the restrooms. On her way, Sofia passed Liam and Emily with tears rolling down her face. She leaned her shoulder on the wall, gazing at the backdoor. Sofia heard footsteps approaching behind her and wiped her eyes.

Liam put his arm around her shoulders. "How are you?"

She shook her head. "I should've pushed harder to date James sooner. Last night, he told me what held him back. I believed that patience was the best approach, because I figured we had nothing but time in front of us."

Sofia paused. "I wish to be with James, but I also want him to be happy. I feel bad for still wanting him when he has a lot of history with her, and she is getting another opportunity at her life. One day can't compare to a four-year relationship that wasn't ended by a breakup. Had the bombing not occurred, they would already be married."

She shook her head. "I understand that this might not seem very important, considering everything that's happening. But right now, this is how I feel."

He gave her a hug. "Everything will be okay."

Liam held her at arm's length. "Sometimes we get timing perfect. I often act too quick or delay too much. It seems you waited too long. Maybe starting a relationship earlier wouldn't have worked out. Maybe you would have a deep commitment to each other. Perhaps he wouldn't have been prepared to commit at that point. It's possible that you would've caused him to flee from your persistence. Even people we care about or want to love hold back information from us. You can't be sure what he was thinking, and you did what you believed was best. He needed every second to work through what happened. For a strong connection to develop, James had to be ready for both of you. Pushing too hard might've been counterproductive towards your end goal."

Sofia nodded. "Maybe you're right."

He chuckled. "My dad would always repeat 'People plan, and God laughs.' I've tried to seize every moment of my life. Once I didn't, and that cost me an opportunity. You never know when opportunities will present themselves again. But when you missed a chance, and it becomes a possibility a second time, make sure you don't miss it twice."

She sighed.

Liam rubbed her shoulder. "A single day can't compare to four years. I won't argue with you on that point or lie and say it doesn't matter. It does. Acknowledging your feelings isn't selfish. You've had a hell of a forty-eight hours. Regardless of what anyone thinks, process your emotions so you can focus on what comes next. On a larger scale, prepare to stop your parents. Bring up your relationship with him when the timing is right."

Sofia gazed at him. *'Will the time ever be right with Jessica back?'* she thought.

Sofia nodded "Okay."

She and Liam observed James and Jessica. Jessica held James' hand between hers.

They both were crying.

James bowed his head.

Sofia turned to Liam. "If you were me, what would you do?"

He held up his fists. "After we finish this, I'd fight for what I want. Seize the moment, remember?"

She smiled. "Do you think I have a chance?"

Liam nodded. "You have a shot, but you must decide if you wish to pursue it."

Sofia focused on him. "What makes you believe that? Robert thinks she's awesome."

He smirked. "You're fantastic too. Besides, I've seen how he looks at you when you don't see him."

Liam patted her on the shoulder, then walked back towards Emily. She grinned until a laugh came from behind her. Sofia turned and saw Roger laughing in the backroom's doorway as he held an ice pack on his testicles.

She crossed her arms. "What's so funny?"

He shook his head. "You're so self-absorbed. With everything going on, you are worried about losing your new boyfriend?"

Sofia glared at him. "You don't know what's happening."

Roger shrugged his shoulders. "Then enlighten me."

She spun. "I don't have a year to waste."

Sofia walked away but froze as a howl sounded outside the store.

Chapter Thirteen

James, Sofia, and Liam exchanged glances in the dim moonlight of the dark store. They walked towards the window behind the counter at the front and surveyed the street. James turned to Liam. "We should leave before those pale creatures return."

Liam nodded. "Agreed. As if the Taken, her parents, and Mr. White weren't enough."

James faced Robert, Jess, Emily, and Roger. "Let's go before more monsters or agents arrive."

Emily, Jessica, and Robert headed for the door.

Roger, moving from the back, threw up his hands. "You two are abandoning me, and I get no thanks?"

Jess and Emily turned.

Emily nodded. "You have a point. Thank you for helping us last night."

Jessica gave a nod in agreement.

Roger chuckled. "At least I'm not the only one getting the shaft in this situation."

Sofia approached him. James held her back. She reached around and flashed her middle finger.

James faced Roger. "You should go too. It's not safe here. The longer you wait, the worse the city will become."

Roger shook his head. "Don't tell me what's best for me. I'm a self-made man. I built myself, and this business. Nothing or nobody can make me run or scare me."

Something pounced through the empty side window frame onto Roger, knocking him to the floor. It bit into his neck and jerked its head back. The creature was a female with desaturated ivory skin under its clothes, and a blood covered mouth. Its glowing white eyes stared at them through its long black hair. Liam raised the pistol and shot it in the skull. It fell on top of Roger. Growls emanated from outside the window and three more creatures jumped inside the store. One female with red hair, and two males with black hair wearing Agency suits. Their physiques were average. They stood and observed James, Robert, and Jess.

Liam screamed. "Hey! Over here!"

The monsters growled as they ran at him. He opened fire on them in quick succession. James and Sofia hurried over and removed the creature from on top of Roger. He held his bloody neck.

James looked up. "Somebody grab something to stop the bleeding."

A chorus of howls emanated in the distance. He stared out the broken window.

With a headshake, Roger grabbed James' left arm. "It's too late for me. Take my other pistol and shotgun from the back, protect your family, and Sofia."

Then his hand dropped. His face fell to the left and his breathing stopped. Liam held out a gun in his hand. James rose and seized it. Liam went to the backroom and returned with a shotgun and another handgun. He extended the handgun to Sofia. She stared at Roger for a second, then took the weapon. Liam led the group from the store. He and James moved towards the left corner to peek down the street. Moonlight illuminated the pale creatures halfway down Fifth Avenue, moving in their direction. James and Liam looked at each other.

James shook his head. "There must be at least fifty thousand of them."

Liam nodded. "Yeah, we need to move now."

Jess grabbed James' right hand as they made their way down Ulysses Street.

Sofia turned to James. "What are those creatures?"

Jess glanced at Sofia. "That's what the spouses from the train became. This must've started with them."

Sofia shook her head. "That would explain why we've seen no people out here tonight."

James nodded. "I thought it was because of the Taken alone. I would've expected more Reapers."

They got to the corner of Ulysses Street and Second Avenue. Ahead of them were six dead pale creatures, two of which were agents. They made their way past and turned right down Second Avenue. Two pale monsters were biting the necks of operatives across the road, with three creatures deceased nearby.

James looked towards the group. "Let's sneak by them. No need to fight or draw attention to ourselves. I'll take the front. Sofia, watch the left. Robert, guard our backs. Liam, monitor the right to track the monsters."

They all nodded and walked down the street. They were five blocks from the campus. The location used to be known as The Point before the city fell into financial troubles. An unknown benefactor purchased the land for triple its already high value. After that, they converted the area into the Allegheny Research Campus. They were three streets away.

James pivoted towards Liam. "What's that group doing?"

Liam turned. "They're still heading the other way."

They were within two blocks.

James glanced over his shoulder. "How's it looking back there Robert?"

Robert peeked behind him. "There's nothing following us."

They were one block from their destination.

James gazed at Sofia. "What's the status on our left?"

She looked towards James. "All clear."

The once wide-open park was now a walled area with one entry point. A ten-foot red brick wall ran along the two sides facing the city. The lack of a barrier by the waterside meant a clear view of the three rivers.

As they got to the entrance, they heard a chorus of HoverCar engines. James spun and saw a caravan of lights come across Southside Bridge. The vehicles veered onto Second Avenue and headed towards them. A choir of howls emanated from the direction of Roger's store.

He waved them forward. "Let's move. That must be more of Mr. White's agents."

They moved into the campus.

Liam pointed to the tallest structure. "What's that building?"

Sofia looked at him. "It's Point Place. They built it where the fountain used to be when this was a park."

Liam nodded. "That's where we are going."

Sofia stared at him. "Why that lab?"

Liam chuckled. "That one dwarfs all the others. It matches your dad's new ego. No offence."

Sofia shook her head. "I can't argue with truth. Follow me, I know the way."

Three buildings stood in front of them. Sofia cut through the middle of two of them. Then she led them under the bridge that remained from its earlier days as a park. Sofia took a right and then stopped. Jess gasped. Emily covered her mouth. Robert put his hands on his head. Liam cursed.

James turned to Sofia. "I guess we know why we haven't seen more Taken in Downtown."

A sea of glowing blue surrounded Point Place. James saw spots of red and yellow as well. Reapers, Thinkers, and Hunters stood between them and their destination. A handful of purple hybrid Evolved Thinkers dotted the crowd as well.

Sofia shook her head. "How are there this many of them? Around my dad's lab was a couple hundred. Now there's about fifty thousand here."

Liam chuckled. "So, let me get this straight. There's about one hundred thousand Taken and those pale creatures. And a convoy of agents headed here?"

He faced the group. "Well, it's been a pleasure knowing you all. James, make sure they bury me in something nice. Oh, and pick me a beautiful casket. If you put me in a plain wood box, I'll haunt you and all your descendants."

James shook his head. "You're not dying here."

He stared at everybody. "Nobody is, understand? We'll get through this. There is more life to enjoy. This is one more hurdle."

Sofia pointed towards the building. "Look."

James turned. Andrea emerged from the front door and headed their way.

Chapter Fourteen

Sofia walked across the massive snowy lawn that led to the Point Place building on the Allegheny Research Campus. The rest of the group followed behind her as they approached the mass of Taken. As they moved, the sirens and the roars of the other creatures grew closer. The Taken stepped aside to create a path for Andrea. Sofia arrived at the front of the throng, staring at the two Reapers standing docile before her. They stepped aside as her mother advanced. Sofia stared into her mother's eyes. Andrea did the same before smiling and opening her arms. Tears flowed down Sofia's cheeks as she ran into Andrea's embrace and hugged her mom.

Andrea wiped her daughter's face. "I have missed you so much over the past year."

Sofia nodded. "I've missed you too."

Andrea sighed. "I was so angry at the people responsible for making me what I am."

She held her daughter at arm's length and looked into her eyes. "I didn't want to become this, but it was necessary for my survival. Revenge consumed my every thought; I didn't realize just how much I'd been missing you until I saw you yesterday."

Sofia grabbed her mother's hand. "We have to go. Mr. White's agents, along with the other creatures, are coming."

Andrea concentrated on her daughter. "What creatures?"

Sofia stared at her. "They're pale, humanlike creatures that eat people. One killed my old boss, Roger. We slipped by them, but there's tens of thousands following The Agency's operatives this direction."

Andrea kissed Sofia on her forehead. "We'll take care of any obstacle. Now that we're reunited, nothing can stop us."

Liam waved both hands in the air. "Except for prison. You and your husband transformed fifty thousand people without their permission, which resulted in deaths, including your daughter's best friend and my... father. Let's not forget that you detonated three EMPs that fried everything with 6G tech in it. That alone caused several millions of dollars in damage. You can't just walk away from crimes against humanity, murder, terroristic acts, destruction of city infrastructure, and residential and commercial properties. They will hold you responsible. I want to turn you into the proper authorities so you two pay for what you have done. Mr. White may to kill you, so I suggest you come with us."

Andrea looked at Sofia.

Sofia nodded. "He's right. You and papa did terrible things and caused many people pain. What you did hurt me, and you must correct it. Your legacy can't be the last three days. All your accomplishments are greater than that. You can fix this."

Andrea's eyes watered. "You're both right. This was never my plan. The events of the past forty-eight hours were all your father's scheme. I should've stopped him, but I didn't. He unleashed this while I stood there."

Andrea turned to Liam. "Once this situation is over, I'll accept responsibility for my complicity and failure to prevent it. I won't put up a fight. But for now, we must prepare for a battle."

She pointed behind them, and they shifted their focus. About one hundred of Mr. White's agents moved towards them. As they rushed toward the Taken, the pale monsters arrived. When the operatives noticed, half of them pivoted to protect their rear. They were about to be sandwiched between over one hundred thousand Taken and pallid creatures. Eight drones descended from the sky and hovered above the agents in a circle. A drone projected the hologram of General Johnson.

The General pointed at Andrea. "It's time for you and Mateo to surrender yourselves and the formula you stole from Mr. White. If nothing else, do it for Sofia."

She stared at Sofia. "You can't steal what you created. We had a deal, and he tried to murder us. An attempt on our lives is sufficient reason to void the contract. We'll turn ourselves in, but not to him. He has already proven that he wants our demise."

General Johnson smiled at Andrea. "He doesn't want you dead right now. Although he might have, situations are fluid. If you give him what he desires and work with him to fix this, he'll forgive you. Don't you want to go back to how life was before this started?"

She looked towards Sofia, who shook her head.

Andrea shifted her attention back to the hologram. "I don't believe you, and I do not trust him. We'll labor to stop this, but not with him."

The General laughed. "You must be mistaken. This isn't a choice. This is an ultimatum that seems like it has options, but it doesn't. There's only one correct answer, and that's yes. Give it to us and join, or else."

She shook her head. "If he wants the formula, tell him to come get it himself."

General Johnson frowned, then his hologram disappeared.

Guns emerged from the belly of the drones.

Andrea turned to the group. "Stand behind me!"

Sofia, James, and the rest ran in back of her. The drones and agents fired on the Taken and the ashen monstrosities who just arrived. Andrea put up an energy shield that caught all the bullets being shot in their direction. Every bullet caused the forcefield to ripple, emitting a white pulse, then rotated in place against the barrier. It protected them, and any Taken positioned behind them, but the fortification wasn't wide enough to protect all the mutants. Blue Reapers, red Thinkers, and yellow Hunters were falling to shots from the drones as other Taken attacked the operatives and the pale creatures. The drones were shooting and switching targets. Andrea turned to a Thinker. She gazed at it. The Thinker nodded and pointed towards the drones. A Hunter and six Reapers gathered. The Thinker guided the Reapers. Three on each side grabbed the Hunter and threw it at a drone that was firing at the sallow monsters. The Hunter landed on the drone and dug its claws into it. It maneuvered the drone toward the other drones. The Hunter controlled drone eliminated six of the others. They exploded on impact, killing the agents and pale creatures in the vicinity. The Hunter's drone and the final drone exchanged rounds. It hit the Hunter in the chest. As the other drone fell, The Hunter ripped out the wiring of its drone. The drone smoked and lost altitude. With the rest of its strength, the Hunter pounced off and a group of Reapers caught it as the last drones detonated on the ground. They laid the injured Hunter on the grass. One Reaper clamped down on its neck. The Hunter writhed as its muscles grew. Its skin changed from yellow to green. It stood up and let loose a high-pitched pulsating roar. The creature faced Andrea.

She pointed her head. "Go, my Slayer. Hunt."

It sped through the operatives, taking down multiple per second with powerful blows. Several of the blanch monstrosities headed right for them. Andrea looked at the nearest Thinker. It roared, and all the Taken in front of her dropped to the ground. She thrust her hands forward and then fell to her knees. The bullets from the drones and agents that she'd suspended accelerated through the creatures and operatives all the way back to the last monsters. She'd eliminated hundreds of them in one move, but thousands remained. The remaining creatures tried to fight past the front line of Reapers and the few Hunters in the crowd while the few Thinkers directed the Taken defense. The lights powered up. A wave of illumination spread throughout the city. When the flood spotlights shone on the long lawn and pathways, the pale freaks under them howled in pain. Their skin reddened as they turned to escape the light. The Taken continued to attack them until they left the campus, fleeing the brightness. When possible, the creatures steered clear of being under the lampposts. The lighting caused hundreds of faded monsters to fall and burst into flames. They flailed and wailed until they went silent.

Sofia turned to help Andrea to her feet. "Are you okay?"

Andrea smiled. "I'm alright. Let us go inside before more creatures arrive. We'll talk to your father. Before more agents arrive, we have a chance to convince him."

Sofia nodded, and they made their way through the remaining Taken towards Point Place.

The building had one hundred floors.

An extra layer of burnt orange wrapped its white exterior on the bottom three levels.

They entered the structure and headed for the GravLifts. The lobby had black framed windows with white walls and burnt orange floor tiles to match the outside.

Andrea turned to Sofia. "I hope you understand I didn't want to trade you for the formula. Leaving the city with you is what I wanted. I want our family to be together again. Your father's decision was his own."

Sofia nodded. "I know mama. Papa's choice isn't important at the moment. The focus is persuading him to cease and correct his actions."

Andrea gave a nod. She and her daughter ascended first. James followed them with Robert on the left and Jess holding his right hand. Liam and Emily watched them rise.

She leaned over to Liam. "The glowing lady with the power is her mom?"

Liam nodded.

Emily looked at Andrea and Sofia in the GravLifts as they approached the top floor. "So, her parents made these creatures? The ones that killed our dads?"

He gazed at her.

She shook her head. "What are you going to do about it?"

Liam glanced at her. "They'll pay for everything they've carried out."

Emily crossed her arms. "It's not fair. They get a chance to atone while they left us parentless."

He rubbed her back. "This is unfair, but they may be the only ones who can fix their mess fast enough to make a difference. Mr. White's scientist might discover it, but he doesn't strike me as the type to not use the research for his benefit as well. Like it or not, we need them right now."

She shook her head. "I second your dislike, for the record. What if they can't undo this?"

Liam stared at her. "Then we're screwed."

They entered the GravLifts and ascended to the top floor.

Chapter Fifteen

Andrea and Sofia exited the GravLift and landed in the lab on the top floor. Reapers, Hunters, and Evolved Thinkers stood near the white walls. Past the nine metal tables set up in rows of three with research equipment, Mateo looked out the ShadeGlass window. "Why did you help them?"

He turned to Andrea.

She shook her head. "What do you mean why? Our daughter was out there with Mr. White's agents, drones, and thousands of other creatures that would've killed her. The people who have kept her alive from your path of destruction also needed our help."

Robert landed with James and Jess, who were still holding his hands.

Mateo scoffed. "She went with them, siding against her blood. A day later, he is grasping another woman's palm."

He turned to Sofia. "That's what happens when you side against your kin. Life knocks you off your high horse."

Liam and Emily touched down behind the group.

Sofia marched towards her father. "I would oppose the President if she was wrong."

Mateo stared into her eyes. "You should always stand by loved ones."

She shook her head. "The man who stands in front of me isn't worthy of loyalty, especially when it's not shown to anyone but himself. We want you to fix what you have done. So does Mr. White, and I'm sure he won't ask as nicely. Turn yourselves in to the authorities and stop this."

He sucked his teeth. "You have always had your mother's naivety. She may have been able to move on from what happened in our youth, but I didn't. This business with Mr. White reminds me of that. I won't yield to a wolf, regardless of its size or ferocity. Converting the terrorists into my Reapers, Thinkers, and Hunters gave me power I hadn't experienced since I killed the men who murdered my family."

Sofia covered her mouth.

Mateo pointed at her. "That reaction is why I never told you. I tried to forget about the helplessness of being the victim. To put aside the memory of how great it felt to avenge my parents. I was too young to understand my emotions towards it. Should I feel guilty about what I've done? Or was I justified? Was I a good person for ridding the world of those murderous drug dealers? Or was I as evil as them for taking their lives? They killed countless people. Your mother feels guilt over the man she slew."

She laughed. "Mama isn't a killer."

Sofia turned and saw her mother's eyes full of tears.

She shook her head. "That's not true, is it?"

Andrea opened her mouth, but no words escaped.

Mateo put his hands behind his back. "He slaughtered her family and raped her sister, but she still harbored feelings of guilt. She felt evil, so she dedicated her life to trying to better the world, as did I. After dealing with the terrorists and Mr. White, I believe killing wickedness is justified and that I remain a good person if I kill the wicked."

Sofia shook her head. "That's a separate issue, but how do you justify transforming people into Taken without their consent? Not everyone was guilty."

He laughed. "Nobody is innocent. Some individuals just don't get caught. Whether it's significant or trivial. Some employees steal pens from work, others murder their families. Some criminals launder money, others cheat on their partners."

Mateo turned to James. "Speaking of which, who's your new lady? Twenty-four hours ago, you were fighting to save Sofia from me. How dare you hurt my daughter like that?"

James shook his head. "This is my fiancée whom I presumed dead in the same bombing Sofia thought you died. Unlike you, she fought to get back to me, while you created monsters to seek revenge instead of returning to Sofia. Don't you even think about judging me or speaking about things while uninformed."

Sofia walked up to her father. "Why was it so easy for you to trade me for that formula?"

Mateo looked into Sofia's teary eyes before turning and walking behind a table.

He cleared his throat. "This is about more than you. I am improving humanity. Making people stronger and eliminating our differences. I'm enhancing society by removing the tyrants."

Liam chuckled. "Yeah right. You don't even believe that. This isn't about any of that. The world and its population mean nothing to you. This is all about your ego. My father died at the hands of your Reapers. Your Hunter killed her dad."

Mateo turned and smiled.

Liam aimed his pistol. "If you start a monologue, your new name will be Ichabod."

Mateo's smile transformed into a scowl.

Liam lowered his gun. "You are trying to destroy everything and set yourself up to be a tyrant. Mutating individuals against their wishes doesn't make this planet better. They may look similar, but you are not eliminating any differences, you're making them even more dangerous. Those disparities only disappear if every single person around the globe transforms into a Taken, but that won't happen. Good people are always going to stand in your way."

Mateo crossed his arms. "You're as narrow minded as Mr. White, General Johnson, and Colonel Brian. After I dispose of your group of overachievers like I did your father, there's only one more person standing in my path."

Liam tried to rush him, but James, Robert, and Emily held him back.

After he calmed down, he pointed at Mateo. "You're lucky that we need you alive, or you'd already be dead."

Mateo clapped. "Bravo James. Another decent job playing hero. Thank you for saving Liam from himself. If you want to be a savior, convince your group to join me. Together, we'll save humanity."

James shook his head. "Joining you is out of the question. Doing the right thing is the only thing. This is not the right thing."

Mateo looked around. "I'm disappointed in all of you. Don't you understand the need for my actions? If I succeed, the differences that have always divided humankind will be gone. We'll live in peace with no corruption because of material things. Is that not paradise?"

James stared at him. "Choice is paradise. Living under the control of one person's whims is pure hell."

Mateo pointed to Andrea. "She will rule by my side. Andrea is wise council to help lead us into the future as my queen."

She scoffed. "You haven't listened to me since Mr. White's betrayal. Not when you detonated bombs in the sky, nor when you unleashed the Taken, and not about Sofia. I don't want to be a ruler of slaves, nor should you wish to be their king. Our families were completely controlled by the rule of drug kingpins that took their lives. How can you not see you have become what we escaped?"

Mateo slammed his fist on the table. "I'm nothing like them. You should know that better than anyone. They killed innocents with their drugs. No narcotics or death in my world. There will only be evolution."

He scanned the room. "It appears everyone here is against me. The hero, his brat, and his lover. The orphan twins and my naïve daughter. And last, my ungrateful wife."

Andrea marched over and slapped Mateo. He grabbed his left cheek and slowly turned around to look at her.

His face was red, and his eyes were fiery. "I've had enough. For decades, my main concern has been you two and advancing the world. You have always supported that goal. I have figured out how to achieve it with a flawless technique, and because you do not agree with my methods, you have abandoned me."

Mateo wagged his finger. "I won't let Mr. White, them, Sofia, or even you hinder my progress any longer."

He peered past Andrea to a Hunter. It looked at one of the Evolved Thinkers.

The Thinker stared at Mateo and shook its head. "No."

Andrea glanced at the Evolved Thinker, then at Mateo. "You would dare try to sic your mutants on us? Creations made from our sweat and tears, from my literal blood."

She took a step backward. "You are not the man I loved anymore. The bombing changed you more than anyone. With me altered and all these Taken surrounding everyone, you're still the biggest monster here."

Her hand shot out, and she psychokinetically lifted Mateo into the air.

Sofia ran to her side. "What are you doing?"

Andrea stayed focused on Mateo. "If he tried to kill us, his only family to carry out this level of evil, then we must stop him."

Mateo chuckled. "What're you going to do? End my life yourself? You don't have it in you."

She shook her head. "That's what I intend to do. Save my daughter and prevent you from ruining the world any further."

A ball of light formed in her hands, and she grasped it. A similar glowing orb encircled him. His smile turned to panic. He gasped for air and pounded against the energy sphere, which flashed brighter on impact. Mateo screamed, but his words were inaudible.

Sofia pulled Andrea's arm. "Please stop! You're killing papa!"

James walked over to Andrea. "Can he undo what he has done?"

She shook her head. "Not without me. That's why he tried to kill me. He wishes to keep it as is."

James nodded. "Are you able to reverse it on your own?"

Andrea gritted her teeth. "No, I can't."

He put his hand on her shoulder. "Then we still need him alive. Have the Reapers restrain him while we figure out what to do next."

The Reapers pulse roared. Shots rang out from behind the group, and they took cover behind the metal workstations. When the gunfire stopped, they looked around the edge to find General Johnson and a team of agents standing there. The Taken laid lifeless with bullets to the head. The General destroyed the GravLift's controls with his fist.

He pointed to James. "You should listen to him. We need you both alive. It would be a shame to kill you because you killed him."

Chapter Sixteen

General Johnson stood near the disabled GravLift.

Isaac, Colonel Brian, and two dozen agents took their positions alongside him.

Liam stared at his dad. "You're alive?!"

Emily looked at Brian. "I thought you were dead."

The General held up his hand. "Now is not the time for pleasantries or reunions. Mr. White wishes to talk to you two, so please set him on the ground."

Andrea released the ball of light, and Mateo dropped to the floor with a thud, gasping for air.

General Johnson nodded. "Thank you."

Mateo stood glaring at her.

Mr. White's hologram appeared, showing him sitting behind his black mahogany desk with a drink in his hand. "Hello Mateo, Andrea, and others. I see a couple fresh faces."

He pointed towards Mateo and Andrea. "You two need to decide. Either bring me the Evolution formula and join me to fix your mess, or you face the consequences. You've done things, I've done things, but I'm not an unreasonable man. I can forgive all if you cooperate with me now. The ball is in your court."

She nodded. "I will help repair what's been done. The events of the past two days were not what I desired. I want to undo what happened and live with my daughter."

Mr. White smiled. "What say you Mateo?"

Mateo smirked. "I no longer have the formula, and I refuse to work with you again."

Mr. White set down his glass and folded his hands. "I didn't think you'd do this the easy way. That part comes as no surprise, but what do you mean you don't have the formula?"

Mateo gestured in James' direction. "They took it from me yesterday."

Mr. White turned towards James, Sofia, and Liam; his fingers still intertwined. "Where are the vials of Evolution?"

Liam shook his head. "It's gone Mr. Shite."

Mr. White pinched the bridge of his nose. "Do you know how valuable that was?"

Liam smirked. "I don't care if it turns crap to gold. Neither of you needed to have it. You're both crazy. We came here to stop him from making more of it for his nefarious reasons."

Mr. White fumed at Liam before turning back to Mateo. "So, you do not have the formula. Did you make more? Are you willing to produce more?"

Mateo shook his head. "Not for you. You tried to kill us, and now you want me to generate more of it for you? Had you not attempted that, you would have the formula. I understand why you thought it necessary, but you were mistaken. This situation is your fault."

Mr. White took a gulp of bourbon and set down the glass. "I had my reasons for trying to eliminate you. It seems I made the correct choice. That could be water under the bridge if you want."

He studied Mateo. "Are you willing to help us undo what has been done?"

Mateo shook his head. "No, and she can't do it without me, so go drown in that water under your bridge."

Mr. White leaned over his desk. "So, you won't aid me. Andrea cannot fix this on her own, and they don't have the formula. Did I get all of that correct?"

Mateo nodded.

Mr. White picked up his glass. "General, kill them all except for the two targets. Bring them to me alive."

General Johnson removed his weapon from its holster.

Isaac pulled his gun and pointed it at the left side of the General's head. "What are you doing Mr. White? You promised nothing would happen to Liam."

Mr. White placed down the glass. "That was before he and his cohorts destroyed an invaluable formula. Plus, your son irks me."

The rest of the agents aimed their weapons at Isaac.

Liam directed his shotgun at General Johnson, while James and Sofia targeted the other agents.

Colonel Brian held his hands out to diffuse the situation. "Everybody just take a second to breathe. Mr. White, those are civilians over there. No need to spill more innocent blood."

Mr. White smiled. "Who, except babies, are guiltless? Aren't we all guilty of something? As for Isaac and Liam, Captain Smith is making his choice. Plus, I am not fond of Liam. The rest of them stole and destroyed invaluable property. Now do as you're told. Retrieve the two targets and kill the rest, including Isaac."

Colonel Brian removed his gun from its holster and pointed it at the agents.

Mr. White held up his hand. "Don't do this Brian. Take a moment and consider it. Think about Emily. By doing this, you put her in danger."

The Colonel turned to his daughter, and she nodded.

He looked at Mr. White's hologram. "You've forced me to choose this side."

Mr. White pounded both fists onto the desk. "Deal with this General."

General Johnson slammed his cybernetic arm into Isaac and his right fist into the back of Brian's head.

As they hit the ground, Andrea stepped forward and struck the General and the operatives with a blast of energy, sending them flying backward.

Three of the agents plummeted down the GravLifts shafts to the lobby.

Brian and Isaac rushed toward Liam and Emily, taking cover behind the middle metal table in the front.

James, Robert, and Jess were behind the right workstation in the center row. Andrea stood between both tables. The remaining operatives shot at her. She produced an energy shield that pulsed with white light when each bullet impacted it, causing the bullets to rotate upon colliding with the shield. Everybody ducked low as possible. A chorus of roars emanated from outside the building. The first group emptied their magazines and reloaded while the second fired at her.

General Johnson chuckled from cover as he heard the symphony of shots. "We can do this all night. I brought enough ammo on the HoverCopter to destroy all your Taken. Before they arrive, all the non-essentials will die."

James saw Andrea's feet slip. '*She needs our help.*' he thought.

He turned to Liam. "She's losing grip. Andrea can't keep this up much longer. We need to help her so she can let those bullets fly."

James pointed to Isaac, Liam, and Colonel Brian. "You three go left. Sofia and I are going right."

Isaac and Brian moved to cover and hit two of the agents. Two more operatives fired at their position, forcing the Colonel and Isaac to duck behind the left metal table in the rear. As the agents reloaded, Liam whistled to get their attention. They hurried to finish reloading, but he shot twice. The operatives fell motionless while more turned towards Liam. He ducked down as they advanced, but the agents sought refuge when Isaac and Colonel Brian provided suppressing fire.

James hit three operatives while Sofia struck two in the chest. The agents returned gunfire, and they crouched.

Jess, Robert, and Emily moved to the back right metal workstation in the rear corner near the windows.

Robert watched anxiously, first observing Liam's battle before focusing on his father's shootout. His gaze shifted left and caught Mateo making a dash for an exit, holding a small case.

Robert swung around to his dad again and pointed. "Mateo is trying to escape!"

Liam moved to give chase, but a bullet passing by his head forced him to retreat into cover. Isaac hit the agent who fired at Liam.

Andrea, soaked with sweat, gazed at Mateo. "Please help us."

He turned and stared at her. General Johnson shot Mateo in the shoulder, causing him to spin and fall to the ground. Andrea let out a yell and turned in the General's direction. She thrust her arms forward, and the bullets flew toward General Johnson and his agents. The General evaded, but their own ammunition hit his men. Andrea fell to the floor in exhaustion. General Johnson peeked over the table at her on both knees.

He turned to his agents. "Kill them now."

The operatives raised their guns, but Andrea ripped them from their hands and crushed the remaining firearms into a metal ball before collapsing face first onto the ground.

Isaac and Brian fired their final rounds at the General.

He used his cybernetic arm to guard his head, forming an energy shield.

Bullets ricocheted to the sides, shattering the exterior windows.

General Johnson looked at his new limb. "Look at that."

Liam ran to catch him by surprise. The General backhanded Liam with the shield, sending him flying across the lab. James and Sofia unloaded their magazines at General Johnson, but their last shots did not damage his cybernetics or shield. More roars echoed from the stairwell. The Taken were making their way up the hundred and two flights towards them.

The General pointed to the agents. "Finish them now. We need to leave before those monsters arrive."

The operatives moved forward and attacked. Colonel Brian and Liam held their own against the agents as they traded blows. Isaac, however, was struggling, missing more than he landed. Despite taking a beating, Sofia avoided a punch and positioned herself behind the female agent. She grabbed the agent's hair and yanked hard, slamming her head into the ground. The woman's head cracked upon impact with the floor. The agent clasped her skull before her hands fell limp.

James was also losing his fight, avoiding the first blows but not the next strikes. An agent punched James with an overhand right, doubling him over in pain and dropping him to his knee. The agent kicked him in the stomach so hard he flipped onto his back. The agent mounted him and pulled out a knife, trying to push it towards James' heart. He used both hands to keep the blade at bay, but it edged closer to his sternum. James kneed the agent in the testicles, turned the dagger and drove it into the agent's chest. The man fell to the side.

He sat up, seeing his child breathing heavily while looking at the dead agent. James reached out. "It's alright. I'm okay."

As he stood, an agent pushed Robert through the empty window frame. James ran and dove out after his son. Jess yelled and extended her arms towards them as Emily held her back. An agent faced them and moved closer as they retreated.

Sofia sprinted to the agent with fiery eyes and a scowl on her face. Then her feet left the ground, and she glided. Sofia's right hand glowed bright yellow. The agent noticed the light and looked at her as she rushed toward him, readying himself for a collision. Sofia punched the agent in the chest, sending him flying out of the building through another opening. He descended and landed in the river.

Everyone stopped fighting and stared at her.

As she turned, the same yellow energy that had enveloped her fist spread across her entire body.

Mr. White's hologram appeared. "You didn't destroy the Evolution formula, you took it."

Sofia looked at her hands, then peered at Mr. White.

He turned to General Johnson. "Capture the women, find Mateo, and kill the rest. The Evolution formula belongs to me, and I'll have it by any means."

The General nodded and Mr. White disappeared. Andrea stood up as Sofia walked beside her.

General Johnson waved them over to him. "Come with us peacefully. Please don't make this hard."

Andrea shook her head. "I was willing to before he tried to kill my daughter. Now, I'm choosing the hard way."

The General shrugged. "Suit yourself."

Sofia raised her fists and moved to the right. General Johnson lifted his hands and his eyes darted between them. Andrea pushed her palms forward, hitting him with an energy blast that struck his right arm. He swung toward her, but Sofia glided over and punched the left side of his face. The General spun and stumbled backward a few feet, dropping to one knee. He rose and turned around, wiping the blood from his mouth. General Johnson glanced at the crimson stain on his cybernetic arm. "That was a mistake, Sofia."

The General approached her. Andrea threw another energy blast at him. This time, he turned his body, catching the attack with his cyber shield. The energy circled his bionic enhancement. Sofia attacked from his right, and a left jab from General Johnson sent her flying across the lab. She smashed into the wall and fell to the floor with a thud. Jess and Emily came up to her.

Sofia held up her hand. "I'm fine. Just stay back."

She stood up and laughed. "That didn't even hurt. Is that the best you got?"

The General chuckled. "We've only started."

Liam, Isaac, and Brian resumed fighting the agents. The Colonel took a beating as his fight recommenced. Liam traded punches with his opponent, while Isaac once again swung and missed. Isaac threw a right hook, but the agent ducked under it and caught him with an uppercut, sending him flying back. The agent pounced on him and grabbed his throat. Isaac raked at the man's eyes until the agent extended his arms, putting his face out of Isaac's reach. He punched the agent's limbs, but his reduced strength did little.

Liam landed a punch to the liver, doubling his opponent over in pain. He turned and saw his father being strangled. In the blink of an eye, he knocked the agent off his dad.

Liam looked back to where he had stood a split-second prior.

A red trail led from his earlier position to his current one.

Red energy engulfed him, starting from his feet up to his head. Isaac gasped for breath.

He looked at Liam with a mix of emotions. "You took that formula too?"

Liam nodded.

Isaac shook his head. "What were you thinking? What if it had killed you?"

Liam extended his hand to help his dad up off the ground. "Good thing for you it didn't."

Isaac stood, and Liam held up a finger. "One second."

In the next few seconds, he repeatedly punched the remaining three agents until they lay unconscious on the ground.

He arrived back at his father's side before Isaac knew what had happened. "You were saying?"

Colonel Brian spun in confusion until he noticed Liam.

Andrea and Sofia were sweating and panting from their fight with General Johnson.

Brian glanced at Liam. "Wanna help your friends out? They need it."

Mr. White's hologram appeared and stared at Liam. "You too?"

Liam nodded. Mr. White turned to the General. "You can just collect his blood. If you bring him back alive, I'll kill him myself."

Mr. White's hologram disappeared.

Liam shook his head. "And here I thought we made progress."

He walked to Sofia's left side. Andrea stood to her right.

General Johnson chuckled. "You're going to need more help than this if you think you can defeat me."

A blue glow from the right blinded everyone. They turned towards the window. James hovered outside it with Robert on his back smiling.

Jess covered her mouth and wept. James smiled at her. He turned and exchanged smiles with Sofia, and nodded to Liam.

James pointed at General Johnson. "They have it."

Chapter Seventeen

James glided from the night sky with Robert on his back, through the shattered window and landed in the lab between Liam and Sofia. His son dropped and ran across the white tile floor to Jess. She pulled him close and kissed his forehead. James smiled as he saw her embrace his child, then turned his attention to General Johnson. Liam leaned over to James. "I want to fly. So... switch powers with me?"

The General cleared his throat. "I will defeat all of you, regardless of your numbers or power."

James shook his head. "You can't beat us because you battle on behalf of a black-hearted man that would sacrifice even you to accomplish his goals. We fight for each other, and for our loved ones. You cannot defeat us, because our motivation is stronger than yours."

Isaac and Colonel Brian walked beside Liam.

Mr. White's hologram appeared. "You think I'm evil?"

James nodded. "I call it like I see it."

Mr. White smiled. "If you knew the things I've done to protect the United Continents of America, you would praise me. The U.C.A. and their cities have been moments away from destruction multiple times. Every time, we have opposed the malicious forces to protect you. There has never been a parade for the secret wars we've won. No monument for the agents who died, and that's okay. I didn't start this office for recognition. The Agency operates in dark places that society wants to believe don't exist. It's designed to slay the boogeymen so the countries can have sweet dreams. Think of me as you wish. I know who I am, and I do not need your approval or validation. You should help me thwart the Taken instead of impeding my progress. With General Johnson leading you, we have the power to put an end to the Taken, those creatures, and anything else thrown at us."

Sofia shook her head. "My mother could control the Taken. Your involvement is unnecessary to do this. We will handle this on our own."

Mr. White scanned the surroundings. "Where are these Taken that she controls? Where's Mateo?"

Andrea looked at the spot where he fell after being shot. Only a pool of blood remained.

Emily glanced outside, then turned to gaze at them. "They're all gone."

Andrea rushed to the window and examined the exterior of the building.

She sighed. "He must have taken them."

Mr. White nodded. "You thought you had control. It was loyalty. The two are not the same. If he controls even one Taken, it's too many."

He looked from one to the next. "Mateo has power over tens of thousands and has ill intentions for this world. Join forces with me, and with your powers and my leadership, we can impede him and save the planet."

Liam shook his head. "Hell no. I see General Lefty's situation, and I don't want to mirror it. Plus, you've already tried to kill most of us, Andrea twice, so trusting you is out. Our goal is to prevent Mateo from destroying more lives, but we won't do it with your help. We'll handle it ourselves and turn him over to the proper authorities."

Mr. White smiled. "How's that going for you? He escaped with an army."

Liam pointed at Mr. White. "That's because you and your meddling agents interfered. Your past success doesn't make you the sole or ideal choice for this task."

James held up his hand. "Instruct the General to step aside. We must pursue Mateo before he flees."

Mr. White stood there for a moment, studying him.

He turned to General Johnson. "Aid them in capturing him and bringing the Taken under the control of Andrea."

The General stared at him. "No."

Mr. White narrowed his gaze at General Johnson. "That was not a request. It was an order. Mateo's control over the Taken isn't our only concern. We must also put an end to The Pallid."

Colonel Brian scratched his head. "The Pallid?"

Mr. White turned to Brian. "The pale zombie-like creatures. Thwarting the Pallid remains necessary, despite Andrea's potential power over the Taken. They're a much larger threat because nobody controls them. The Pallid kill, infect, and transform with no restriction. These four are essential to overcome the threat."

General Johnson pointed at Andrea. "That woman tried to take my life twice, and you're asking me to ally with her?"

He chuckled. "You want to give her authority over those creatures that killed Brian? Seriously?"

Mr. White nodded. "Yes, that's what I want."

Liam stepped forward with a finger raised. "To be fair, you attempted to blow her up with a rocket first."

The General pointed at the group. "I won't work with them again. I can finish this mission on my own. They are unnecessary for me to succeed."

Mr. White stared at General Johnson. "You take orders from me. If you do not obey these commands, you will suffer the repercussions."

The General flashed his middle finger at him. "Here's what I think of your consequences and your agency. I am going to have my revenge, and then I'm coming for you."

Mr. White sighed. "You don't know the ramifications of this decision. I have exhausted all my agents, drones, and resources at my disposal to find Mateo before you let him escape."

He looked at all of them. "Regardless, I aim to block his plans, the Taken, and The Pallid, with or without you."

Mr. White's hologram disappeared.

General Johnson glared at Andrea.

She held up a hand. "Mr. White is right. We must catch him. He's not who he used to be. Mateo's demeanor has grown more hateful and jaded. We can't let him control the Taken by himself. I don't trust Mr. White after he tried to kill me, Oliver, but I still believe you can put the continents before our problems. Are you willing to help us in preventing Mateo's actions?"

The General shook his head. Andrea sighed, then reared back and thrust a blast of energy into General Johnson's chest. The impact sent him flying onto his rear end a few feet away. General Johnson rose and charged toward her until Liam, circling around, delivered one quick blow after another. The General held out his left arm and clotheslined him. Liam hit the floor and slid into the wall. Emily sprinted over to check on him. General Johnson stepped towards Andrea. Sofia glided at him with a right hook of her own. He blocked it with his cybernetics and backhanded her with the absorbed energy from her punch. She went tumbling over multiple workstations. Robert and Jess checked on her. As the General smirked, James flew at him full speed and punched him in the sternum with both fists. General Johnson flew backwards from the impact. He crashed into the wall, then landed face first. The General stood up and grabbed his upper body.

James held up his hands. "We would rather not harm you. You helped us when we needed it. The Agency took our group in like an extended family, and we appreciated it. We all have one goal, and that's surviving. Finishing the mission is necessary. This is wasting our time. Help us or get out of our way so we can finish it."

He held out his hand. General Johnson walked up to James, holding his chest. He stared at James' palm, then into his eyes before delivering a left uppercut that sent him tumbling through the air. James spun out of control as he spiraled towards the high industrial ceiling. He corrected his rotation and hovered near the roof.

The General strolled toward Andrea. "You'll pay now for all that you've done to me."

He swung his cybernetic fist at Andrea's face. She lifted her hand, straining to keep it hovering just in front of her skull. The General tried to grab her, but Isaac and Brian grabbed hold of him. Sofia and Liam seized his enhanced arm.

James landed on General Johnson's left side and examined his augmented limb, looking for a vulnerability. '*There seems to be no weakness.*' he thought.

As Liam and Sofia pulled, the General's appendage clicked and seemed to stretch.

James clutched General Johnson's shoulder and yanked.

The General shook his head. "What are you doing? Stop it!"

General Johnson strained to get free. With one last pull, General Johnson's cybernetic arm popped from its socket. James, Sofia, Liam, and Andrea exchanged looks. Colonel Brian walked over to General Johnson, who stared at his detached limb in James' hand.

The General stared up at the Colonel. "Why would you betray us?"

Brian frowned. "Your change in perspective made it easy to do the right thing."

He paused for a second. "You know you're like a brother to me, but in this situation, you are wrong. I can't stand by and let innocent individuals get hurt, no matter who's trying to harm them."

General Johnson spat at his feet. "It seems you decide when to act heroic. You weren't concerned about the terrorist's family we targeted with their missile."

Brian shook his head. "You made that call. I didn't start the launch, we attempted to halt it. This is way different. Trying to kill people who are attempting to assist is unforgivable. They're civilians, not enemies of the state."

The General stood upright.

James, Liam, and Sofia stepped closer behind Colonel Brian.

General Johnson poked the Colonel in the chest with his right hand. "Without the ability to tackle hard tasks, you are unworthy of wearing this suit."

Brian took off his jacket and dropped it on the floor in front of General Johnson. "You can have it. Soldiering or being an agent entails more than doing hard tasks. It's also about doing the right things."

He turned and walked away.

James approached the General and locked eyes with him. "Let's talk."

The others surrounded them.

He folded his hands. "What did Mr. White plan to do if you failed?"

General Johnson stayed silent and continued looking at him.

James held out a hand. "We are trying to stop Mateo and turn things back to normal. Help us finish this fight."

The General persisted in staring.

Mr. White's hologram appeared. "He doesn't know. That big of a decision is between me and one other person. I tried to avoid it, but you all and Mateo have left me with no choice."

James walked over to the virtual image. "What are you planning to do?"

Mr. White puffed his cigar and exhaled smoke. "Save you."

James folded his arms. "How will you be saving us?"

Mr. White took another puff and blew out the smoke. "By any means necessary."

He studied James' eyes. "This whole situation has become about more than the Taken outbreak. The continents' fate is in jeopardy if we don't stop them or the Pallid."

James shook his head. "Our power can stop Mateo, and Andrea can control the Taken. Once she is in command, between that force and our new powers, we can finish the Pallid."

Mr. White drew another puff and exhaled. "What if you fail? That's more time wasted, and lord knows it's a luxury that we don't have. The Pallid emerged as a threat from nowhere and now threaten every human."

James contemplated for a moment.

He looked at Sofia, Liam, and Andrea before turning back to Mr. White. "What if we win? Wouldn't it be better to prevent millions from becoming Taken or Pallid?"

Mr. White nodded. "It would've been more desirable had you not rejected my original offer. You and General Johnson made tough decisions for me by dismissing our second to last hope."

Mr. White put out his cigar. "Don't worry. I will save everyone."

James exchanged looks with Robert, Jess, and Sofia.

He turned back to Mr. White. "You still haven't said how you'll protect everybody."

Mr. White shook his head. "And I won't until you're willing to listen."

His hologram disappeared. All eyes were on James as he spun.

Liam walked over to him and placed his hand on his shoulder. "So, what's the plan buddy?"

James looked around. "I don't know."

Chapter Eighteen

A breeze blew in through the shattered windows. Robert sat on a metal stool in the science lab, head down, elbows resting on his knees, and hands folded. James walked over, took a seat next to him, and rubbed his back. Robert looked up. "I'm sorry."

James chuckled. "Why are you apologizing?"

Robert nodded towards the window. "For not being more alert. I was so anxious about losing you after mom's death that I hesitated to help earlier. When you were fine, I was so relieved that I didn't see the agent coming."

James shook his head. "You have no reason to apologize. I can understand the anxiety of almost losing a second parent. Had you not been in danger, I might not have activated my powers and saved you."

They exchanged smiles until Robert's look turned to curiosity. "How did you know they would activate?"

James shrugged. "I didn't. Taking the formula was a failure in my mind."

He looked at his son. "When I saw you being thrown through the glass; I had no plan. I jumped after you, since there was no time to waste. You were getting closer to the ground. I asked God to save you."

Robert smiled at the heavens.

He shook his head. "How are we going to stop Mateo, the Taken, and the Pallid?"

James shrugged. "I'm not sure yet, but we'll find a solution. We must."

Robert stared at his dad. "Why do we have to? We didn't ask for this."

James glanced around and stopped his gaze on Jess. "Life chose us to be here. We fight to save not just the city or the world, but also ourselves. This is much bigger than us, and it's crucial that we embrace it. Ignoring it will cause our group more harm than good. When you are called and you see what must be done, you do it. Even in the face of danger."

Robert looked at his father with a frown. "I wanted Mateo to pay for what happened to mom. We need him to make a cure quicker. I understand that, but I wish he'd pay for all the people he hurt with the Taken. Does me wanting him to die mean I'm a bad person?"

James shook his head. "You're just human. It's normal to want revenge when others wrong you, or someone you love. The difference between being good or evil is if you act on those impulses. You're not terrible for having negative thoughts. A single thought does not define your identity. Let go of this anger, or you risk it consuming and changing you for the worse."

James set his hand on Robert's shoulder. "I understand you're upset about your mom, but we need a cure soon to prevent other kids from going through the same thing."

Robert nodded and hugged his dad.

****

Sofia saw her mother standing by the GravLifts and walked over to her. "I see you are ready to go. Everybody is catching their breath for a moment. Once they're done, we'll get back to it."

Andrea smiled. "I'm not staying with the group."

Sofia's brow furrowed. "Why? As a team we're stronger, and we just reunited. We should all stick together."

Andrea grabbed her shoulders and looked into her eyes. "I need to go after Mateo myself. He left us when we needed his help. I want answers for his actions. Who he is at present disappoints me. Perhaps if I'm alone, I can get through to him."

Sofia frowned. "What makes you think you can now if you couldn't earlier?"

Andrea sighed. "It's possible that he is still the man I love beneath the hate. If I can reach him… somehow… then we'll stop what's happening and save him from Mr. White's wrath."

Sofia grabbed Andrea's hands. "What if you can't? What if he tries to use the Taken to hurt you again?"

Andrea shook her head. "They won't harm me. He created them from my blood. They can… sense that. That's why they're conflicted about assaulting me."

Sofia nodded. "Them attacking you is not my concern. I'm worried what you might do to papa if he commands it. He lacks powers or super strength, and you are powerful enough to kill him."

Andrea frowned. "I hope it won't happen, but the chances of his return are higher if I go alone. Maybe with one person at the most."

Sofia looked at her mother. "You want me to join you?"

Andrea nodded. "It's possible that your father will be more willing to help if we're both present."

Sofia crossed her arms. "We shouldn't leave without everyone else. I don't think papa is going to change his mind."

Andrea stared at James. "Are you trying to keep us all together because of him?"

Sofia pointed to her head. "No, it's the smarter strategy."

She looked at him. "If I went with you and something happened to James, Robert, or Liam, I'd never forgive myself. We've protected each other through this so far, and I would hate to fail them because I wasn't there."

Andrea caressed Sofia's face. "Make the choice that's best for you. Talk to James if you must. If you decide to stay with them, I understand. I've made my decision. I'll wait in the lobby for a few minutes for you before leaving. Whatever you choose, I love you more than anything in this world. You'll always be mi Princesa."

They exchanged smiles, and Andrea stepped back into the GravLifts and floated towards the main entrance. Sofia turned around and saw James hugging Robert. Jessica was sitting at a metal table, looking out the shattered window. Sofia took a deep breath and walked up to James.

She touched Robert on the shoulder. "Can I speak with your dad for a moment?"

He nodded. "Of course."

Robert strolled over and sat next to Jess.

James grabbed a seat and looked at Jess talking to Robert. "I know what you're thinking."

Sofia sat down beside him. "You do?"

James gave a nod. "I've been thinking about the same thing. What do I do now that she's returned?"

He stared at Sofia. "To be honest, I'm not sure. There's no handbook for this situation. If I resume my relationship with her, I hurt you. If I choose you, I devastate her."

James grabbed her hands. "I told her we are together. Jess accepted I moved on, but she also wants to pick up where our relationship paused. Jess said the idea of getting back to me kept her going, and she won't stop now because I started over without knowing the truth."

Sofia nodded. "I can't blame her. You're a great guy. I'd do the same in her shoes."

James squeezed her hands. "I didn't ask you out earlier because of reasons unrelated to you."

She smiled. "I know. Whatever you decide to do, I'll live with it if you promise we can stay friends. I experienced a few traumatic life events with you right by my side. Plus, you, Liam, and I are a superhero group now."

James chuckled. "What about your mom?"

Sofia grinned. "She's the misguided half-Taken who will become a hero."

James smirked, but it faded. "So, if I choose Jess, you wouldn't hate me?"

She looked at him. "No, I would not. In life, we rarely get second chances on this scale. I would understand either choice. This whole situation is crazy. We both had people we assumed were dead reappear in our lives."

James beamed again. "Thanks for being understanding. I won't decide until after the mission is done. We still have a mission to focus on after we rest for a bit."

Sofia nodded. "Take all the time you need. I'm not in a rush for a decision."

James looked out the window. "Do you have any idea where your dad might have gone?"

She put her hands on her hips. "I don't know, but I wish I did. This nightmare needs to end. I want my parents to be as they were, but much has changed since the bombing. The biggest being that my father doesn't seem interested in being a husband or dad anymore."

James smiled. "I would've liked to have met him before all this. When Mateo was the man you remember and cherish."

He sighed. "How do we find him?"

Sofia shrugged.

James grinned. "Don't worry Sofi, we'll find your father and make all this right somehow. Let's talk to Liam and see if he has any ideas in that cop brain of his."

She laughed. "I'll be over in a second."

James stood and went towards Liam. Jessica grabbed his hand as he passed. She pulled him into a seat on her other side. James, Robert, and Jess talked, all smiling. Sofia sighed. Jessica touched James' cheek, and he kept her palm there. Sofia rose and walked past Emily having a conversation with Brian.

She glanced at Emily's expression. *'Em looks concerned.'* she thought.

****

Liam hugged Isaac. "I missed your old bones."

Isaac squeezed his son. "I missed your dumb face."

Liam held his dad at arm's length. "You think I have a dumb face?"

Isaac smiled. "Of course, it runs in the family."

They chuckled.

Isaac set his hand on Liam's shoulder. "I hope you realize I love you."

Liam shook his head. "I do. But why did you risk your life? We would've found another way. If you were alive, why didn't you come back to us? How in the blue hell did you end up with Mr. White and General Nonsense?"

Isaac pointed to his head. "Dumb face, even dumber reasoning. I moved a thousand miles per hour in the wrong direction. With the second wave of Taken advancing towards the garage, I had to act. Protecting you was my priority. I didn't want what happened to Brian to happen to anyone else."

He looked at his son. "So, I sacrificed myself for all of you. I fought with everything I had until one of them pounced on me. When I hit the ground, the force concussed me and destroyed my communicator."

Isaac rubbed his neck. "The Reaper's breath was hot on my neck until an agent shot it in the head. An agent in the squad had medical experience. He checked me for a concussion and any bites from the Reaper."

He shook his head. "The world kept spinning for a while after the medic examined me. Once that stopped, I was going to come in and help, but

General Johnson exited injured. Other agents were carrying Brian's body. I tried to get answers from the General, but he ignored me and moved toward a rocket launcher. Once that plan literally backfired on him, the remaining operatives went to check on him. While I was waiting for my brain to clear, you four left in a HoverVan. I didn't know where you'd gone, so I returned with them."

Liam chuckled. "I took them to the cabin."

Isaac nodded. "That was smart."

He looked at the Colonel. "Brian tried to recruit me to work with Mr. White for over a year. I wanted to honor him and protect you, so I asked The Agency for a job. After seeing things firsthand as an agent, I'm not a fan. The decisions that were made by General Johnson weren't agreeable. I challenged what I saw was improper, even when other agents fell in line. After they laughed at me, ignored me, and threatened me, I knew I was in the wrong place. My place was beside my son, cracking jokes and skulls."

Liam shook his head. "You've never cracked a skull in your life. The only thing you crack are lobsters, or your own bones."

Isaac smirked. "I turned a new leaf when you joined the force. Didn't want to give you the wrong impression."

Liam bellowed. "The only leaf you turned is lettuce when you remove it from your burgers."

They shared a laugh.

Isaac placed his hand on Liam's shoulder. "I did what I believed was right then. I regret that decision and would not repeat it. Fate brought us together again, and I won't leave your side a second time. I hope you can forgive me."

Liam grabbed his father's hand. "Of course I forgive you. You're the only dad I got. Not perfect, but the only one."

Isaac smiled at him before smacking the back of his skull.

Liam grasped his head. "Why'd you hit me?"

Isaac crossed his arms. "Why would you ingest a formula made by the person who created the Taken?"

Liam rubbed his head. "I didn't want to be the only one not doing it."

Isaac smacked his skull again.

Liam massaged his head. "Stop hitting me. I'm a grown man."

Isaac stared at him. "Then act like it. That was a stupid decision on all your parts. You might've died. What about Robert?"

Liam narrowed his eyes. "I gave him explicit instructions. He'd have been fine. Besides, we didn't die. We just lost consciousness for twelve hours."

Isaac swung but missed as his son ducked. Liam gloated, but stopped when Isaac's left hand slapped the back of his skull.

Liam rubbed his head. "We knew the formula's purpose. Our actions were based on what we believed was best. We took a calculated risk. Taking Evolution paid off at the very second we needed it to. We saved everyone this time, including you, and Robert. With Andrea on our side, we can stop Mateo, and defeat the Pallid."

Isaac pulled him into a hug.

Liam's arms dangled. "No way I'm hugging you back after what you've done to my cranium."

Isaac rubbed his son's head.

Liam smacked his dad's hand away.

He pointed at his father. "You're getting reported for child abuse."

Isaac was smirking at him until he saw a concerned look on Emily's approaching face.

He put his hand on her shoulder. "What's wrong?"

Emily looked at Brian. "Has my dad been acting weird?"

Isaac shrugged. "He had some memory lapses earlier, but it's understandable after being resurrected."

She shook her head. "This feels familiar, like before I left. He returned from a mission, and he wasn't himself. I ran away out of fear for my safety."

Isaac looked at Brian. "Why didn't you tell us then?"

Liam chuckled. "That's what I wanted to know."

Emily glared at him. "It's not important. I'm back, but he's still unwell."

She observed Brian. "Did he mention me when I wasn't here?"

Isaac scoffed. "Of course he did."

Emily and Liam both faced him.

Isaac scratched his head. "He definitely mentioned you at one point."

Liam crossed his arms.

Isaac glanced at Liam. "Did he not?"

Liam shook his head. "No, not to me anyway."

He shifted his gaze to her. "I thought he coped with your departure that way. Knowing why you left, and who he worked for, that alters all assumptions."

Emily stared at Brian. "My dad's still not himself. I want answers. If this Mr. White did something to him, maybe we can force him to fix it."

Isaac turned to Liam. "You two find Andrea and see if she'll examine Brian. I'm going to talk to him."

Isaac walked over to Brian, who sat there, lost in deep contemplation. Isaac set his hand on his shoulder. Brian jumped a bit.

Isaac held up his hands. "It's only me. I came to check on you. How are you doing?"

Brian shook his head. "What's the matter with me?"

Isaac smiled at him. "Nothing is wrong with you. You went through the most traumatic event anyone can experience."

He exhaled. "They resurrected you."

Isaac gazed at him. "That's a miracle."

Brian looked at his palms. "Something feels… weird. The past two years are fuzzy, and I can't remember certain events before then."

Isaac waved off his concerns. "You've always had a terrible memory; you just missed a few things."

Brian stood. "No, something is wrong with me."

Isaac started speaking, but Brian held up his hand. "When you brought up Emily earlier, I had no idea who she was. I forgot I had a daughter."

He stared at her. "I've lost time with my child, and I want an explanation."

Brian turned to Isaac. "The only person who can answer that question is Mr. White."

Isaac frowned. "That guy is shady. I wouldn't trust him. Besides, you have Emily here now. Take full advantage of the present."

Brian gazed at the floor. "Em told me what I did. How I acted. How I hadn't recognized her and… pulled a gun on her."

He looked up. "I'll make sure it doesn't happen again. Regardless of Mr. White's trustworthiness, wouldn't you do the same if you and Liam were in this situation?"

Isaac sighed. "You're right. After the mission's over, we'll get the answers, and help you need. I promise."

He held out his hand. Brian grabbed it and they shook.

****

James was talking with Jess and Robert when Liam approached.

Liam cleared his throat. "Hey James, can I talk to you for a minute?"

James turned to them. "I'll be right back."

He stood and walked with Liam to a corner of the lab.

Liam scratched his head. "Brian has Emily worried. The whole resurrected savior act might've fried his circuits worse than they already were. We wanted Andrea to look at him since she's a Neural Programmer. When did you last see her?"

James shook his head. "I saw her earlier."

He looked around. "Maybe Andrea's talking to Sofia."

James chuckled. "Find her, and you'll locate Andrea."

Liam positioned James so his back was to Jess and Robert. "We can't locate either of them. I ran down the steps and searched in front of the building. They're not here."

James stared at him. "I just talked to her. She's gone?"

Liam nodded. "She and Andrea went after Mateo, without wanting to wait for everybody."

James looked at the GravLifts. "We must help them stop him. What if the Taken turn on Andrea? Plus, the Pallid are still out there."

Liam patted James' back. "They're two bad ass women with superpowers. I don't think they need our help. They can handle the Pallid on their own. Also, the Taken showed they won't harm Andrea, so Sofia should be safe."

James shook his head. "She asked what I was going to do since Jess returned. I said I hadn't decided yet, and that I would do so after the mission. Perhaps she doubted me. Does she believe I've already chosen?"

James paused for a second. "Has she decided?"

Liam scoffed. "Don't worry about it. Let's focus on stopping Mateo. We find him, we locate them. Take your time and think. In the meantime, enjoy that Jess returned to your life. It's a big decision that you should thoroughly consider."

James nodded and started walking away.

Liam grabbed his shoulder. "Know that she didn't leave because she doesn't want you. She may have left because she wants you to be happy... even if it hurts her."

James turned to Liam. "How can you be so sure?"

Liam grinned. "Because I've seen the way she looks at you when you don't see her."

James smiled. "Thanks buddy."

Liam slapped his shoulder. "No problem. Jess and Robert need you. So does the United Continents of America. If we don't stop Mateo, the world will be Taken."

James chuckled. "How long have you been working on that?"

Liam laughed. "Too long to admit without being embarrassed."

Smirking, James walked towards the group. "Alright everybody. Time to leave. Andrea and Sofia got a head start on us. We want to catch up to them if possible. The odds are better if we fight together."

Robert glanced around the area. "Why did they leave?"

James shook his head. "I'm uncertain, but the reason isn't crucial. We still have a mission to stop the spread of two threats. If we fail, the continents are in danger. So, let's go be great."

Everybody nodded and proceeded towards the broken GravLift. Jess and Robert walked over to James. James wrapped his arms around them both and floated them to the lobby. Emily jumped on Liam's back, and he sped her down the steps. Isaac and Brian brought up the rear, dragging General Johnson with them down the stairs.

Liam was looking at his watch and tapping his feet when they arrived. "Finally, we can go."

Isaac shot him a look as he panted. "We just walked down one hundred and three flights."

Liam pointed to his back. "I would've given you a piggyback ride if you asked nicely."

Everyone headed towards The Agency's HoverCopter in front of Point Place.

Colonel Brian unlocked it with his voice authorization.

The others boarded while he and Isaac prepared for liftoff.

They ascended into the air before heading toward Downtown Allegheny to search for Mateo.

****

Sofia looked back at the science campus as she floated. "Maybe we should've stayed."

Andrea hovered using her abilities. "With you having superpowers now, we move quicker as just a pair. Besides, what Mateo has done is a family matter. We'll handle your father and convince him to do what's right. He'll make up for abandoning us."

Sofia glanced at her mom. "It's not just a family matter. If we can't stop papa, it'll be a concern that spans across both continents too. We have a better chance of forcing his hand with James and Liam assisting our cause. The dad that we knew is gone. I know you don't want to believe it, but it's true."

Andrea shook her head. "I refuse to accept that. Your father is somewhere in there. He must be. Return and team up with them if you wish. Either way, I will continue searching for him."

Sofia smiled. "I just got you back. Nothing will separate us again."

They exchanged smiles and continued floating above the river.

Chapter Nineteen

Mr. White sat in his dimly lit office behind a massive black mahogany desk. On his right stood two matching bookcases filled with hardcover books on topics like philosophy and strategy. Four identical chairs remained unoccupied across from him, awaiting his top people for situations such as this. Smoke floated in the air from the cigar he just extinguished. Mr. White began pouring a tumbler of bourbon but stopped mid pour. He glanced at the bottle in his hand before forcefully tossing it, causing the glass to shatter on the floor.

Madam President Mary Jackson's holographic form shook her head. "What's wrong, White?"

Mr. White spun around. "I... I didn't see you appear."

He stood and fixed his tie. *I don't want her to witness me like this.'* he thought.

President Jackson raised her hand. "You don't have to be perfect with me. I've seen the best and the worst of you. Now, tell me what is bothering you."

Mr. White dropped his hands to his sides. "Two civilians and a cop stole the formula I had designed. The maker of said concoction also created the Taken and is trying to unleash them on the continents. Not to mention that we have an added danger in the Pallid. The thieves and the Queen Taken, Andrea, refused to help me stop the latter threat. I've lost my top two agents and my newest recruit to desertion, or disobedience. Only two patrolling operatives remain alive after tonight's battle against the Taken, the Pallid, and the traitors, while most of my personnel oversee Plan Charlie."

She rubbed her chin. "Can any of the individuals supervising Plan Charlie be called in to contain the situation?"

Mr. White shook his head. "Their jobs are vital to ensuring Plan Charlie works. They're the last line of defense against the Taken or the Pallid taking over the continents should Plan Delta fail."

President Jackson nodded. "Do you think Plan Delta will be unsuccessful?"

Mr. White placed his hands behind him. "No, I've had the best scientists in the world working on this since the Capital City bombing attempt, just in case we needed something of this magnitude. We have checked the calculations thousands of times and run millions of simulations. Plan Delta is ready. I'm holding out on Charlie and Delta as long as I can."

Madam President Jackson studied Mr. White's face. "I thought Plan Charlie was ready. Why are you delaying?"

Mr. White stared at her. "Hope. Plan Charlie is a green light, but I am hoping they stop Mateo. If they do that, Andrea will have control over the Taken, eliminating the threat."

The President crossed her arms. "Do you trust her?"

Mr. White shook his head. "I don't trust anyone, but I glimpsed a part of the old Andrea once she saw Sofia. She wasn't a concern. He was always the worry. I believe she wants to protect her daughter."

She shook her head. "Even if she controls the Taken, there's still the Pallid to consider. Nobody has power over them. Waiting longer increases the devastation of both threats, leaving nothing to rescue."

Mr. White pounded his fist through his desk. "My sole purpose is to protect others. Every decision I made had that intention. I have always prided myself on being a thorough planner and seeing dangers before they show themselves. The one plan that didn't go to spec resulted in the Taken outbreak. Then there's the Pallid. How did I not see them coming?"

President Jackson frowned. "Nobody is perfect, White, no matter how hard you strive for perfection. You can't stress over what you didn't prevent. Focus on what you can thwart and do better next time."

Mr. White tapped his desk twice with his finger. "I want to fix it this time. There are still several risks with Plan Delta, even if it's initially successful."

She smiled. "I trust you, White, no matter the uncertainties. You are right way more often than you're wrong. Just promise me you are going to start plans Charlie and Delta when you must. If you don't, there won't be a next time."

He nodded. "I will."

President Jackson reached to end the call, but hesitated. "Do you think we are making the correct decision? I know the projections on casualties from the Taken. With the Pallid included, I suspect they're way worse now, but is this the best choice? Is this really the top option?"

Mr. White shook his head. "It's not the best choice, but it gives the United Continents of America its greatest chance to survive long term. We don't have the luxury to create new plans. The clock is also our enemy at present."

Madam President Jackson frowned. "Well, I pray God forgives us for what we must do next."

He nodded. "Me too."

TO BE CONTINUED...

Acknowledgements

Out Now!

The Outbreak: The Survive Saga, Book 1

The Evolution: The Survive Saga, Book 2

Coming 2025!

The Aftermath: The Survive Saga, Book 3

If you enjoyed this book, please leave a review telling others why they should read it. This helps spread the word. Thanks.

Special thanks to the following people: Tina, Miyah, Sammy, Mom, Noelle, Zuri, Chersti, ZeppelinDG, Sandy, Drew, Maddi, Rod, Phil, Kim, Jocelyn, Justin, Lindsey, Rue, Marsha, Dawn, Deb, David, Precious, Daniel, Jeremy, Lamont, Dianne, Donald, Shawndre, Wendy and Jason.